ST. THOMAS MORE SCHOOL
GIFT OF
[redacted]
[redacted]

The Remarkable Voyages of CAPTAIN COOK

Rhoda Blumberg

BRADBURY PRESS NEW YORK
Maxwell Macmillan Canada Toronto
Maxwell Macmillan International
New York Oxford Singapore Sydney

ALSO BY RHODA BLUMBERG

Commodore Perry in the Land of the Shogun

The Great American Gold Rush

The First Travel Guide to the Moon

The Incredible Journey of Lewis and Clark

I want to thank Barbara Lalicki, my talented editor, for her guidance. I am also indebted to James P. Ronda, eminent historian, for reviewing my manuscript and illuminating the past for me through his comments.

Bradbury Press
Macmillan Publishing Company
866 Third Avenue
New York, NY 10022

Maxwell Macmillan Canada, Inc.
1200 Eglinton Avenue East
Suite 200
Don Mills, Ontario M3C 3N1

Macmillan Publishing Company is part of the
Maxwell Communication Group of Companies.

First edition
Printed and bound in the United States of America

Design by Kathryn Parise

10 9 8 7 6 5 4 3 2 1

The text of this book is set in 12 point Bembo.

LIBRARY OF CONGRESS CATALOGING-IN-PUBLICATION DATA
Blumberg, Rhoda.
The remarkable voyages of Captain Cook /
by Rhoda Blumberg. —
1st ed.
p. cm.
Includes bibliographical references and index.
Summary: An account of the historic adventures and achievements of the great British explorer and discoverer of Australia, Hawaii, and other Pacific Ocean lands and peoples.
ISBN 0-02-711682-4
1. Cook, James, 1728–1779—Journeys—Juvenile literature.
2. Voyages around the world—Juvenile literature. 3. Explorers—Great Britain—Biography—Juvenile literature. [1. Cook, James, 1728–1779. 2. Explorers.] I. Title.
G420.C65B55 1991
910'.92—dc20 91-11219

FOR MY CREW

DANIEL, CARLA, ILANA

WILLIAM, MELODICA

GREGORY, AMALIA

DANA, ELIZA

CONTENTS

THE SECOND VOYAGE, 1772–1775

THE THIRD VOYAGE, 1776–1780

King George III and his wife, Queen Charlotte, at the royal palace

1 · AN UNKNOWN CONTINENT

THERE WERE TALES about miserable brutes, ugly giants, and man-eating monsters who lived in the southern part of our globe. There were also stories about kind, beautiful people who dwelled there in luxury on lush, treasure-laden lands. In the eighteenth century, when King George III ruled England, government officials wanted to know the truth about people and places in the "South Seas," a term used to mean "Pacific Ocean."

Geographers were positive that a huge continent could be found in the southern waters of the Pacific or Atlantic oceans. They believed that a vast landmass at the bottom of the world anchored our planet and balanced the weight of Europe, Asia, and Africa in the northern hemisphere. It *had* to be there, or the earth would be so top-heavy it would turn over on itself.[1]

Scholars wrote about the "Southern Continent not yet Discovered," also called the "Great South Land," the "Unknown Southern Continent," and "Terra Australis Incognita." They scrutinized old maps showing bays, rivers, and mountains on a land no human being had ever seen. And they studied newer maps that featured a continent circling the bottom of the earth, extending into warm and temperate climate zones close to South America, Asia, and Africa. Al-

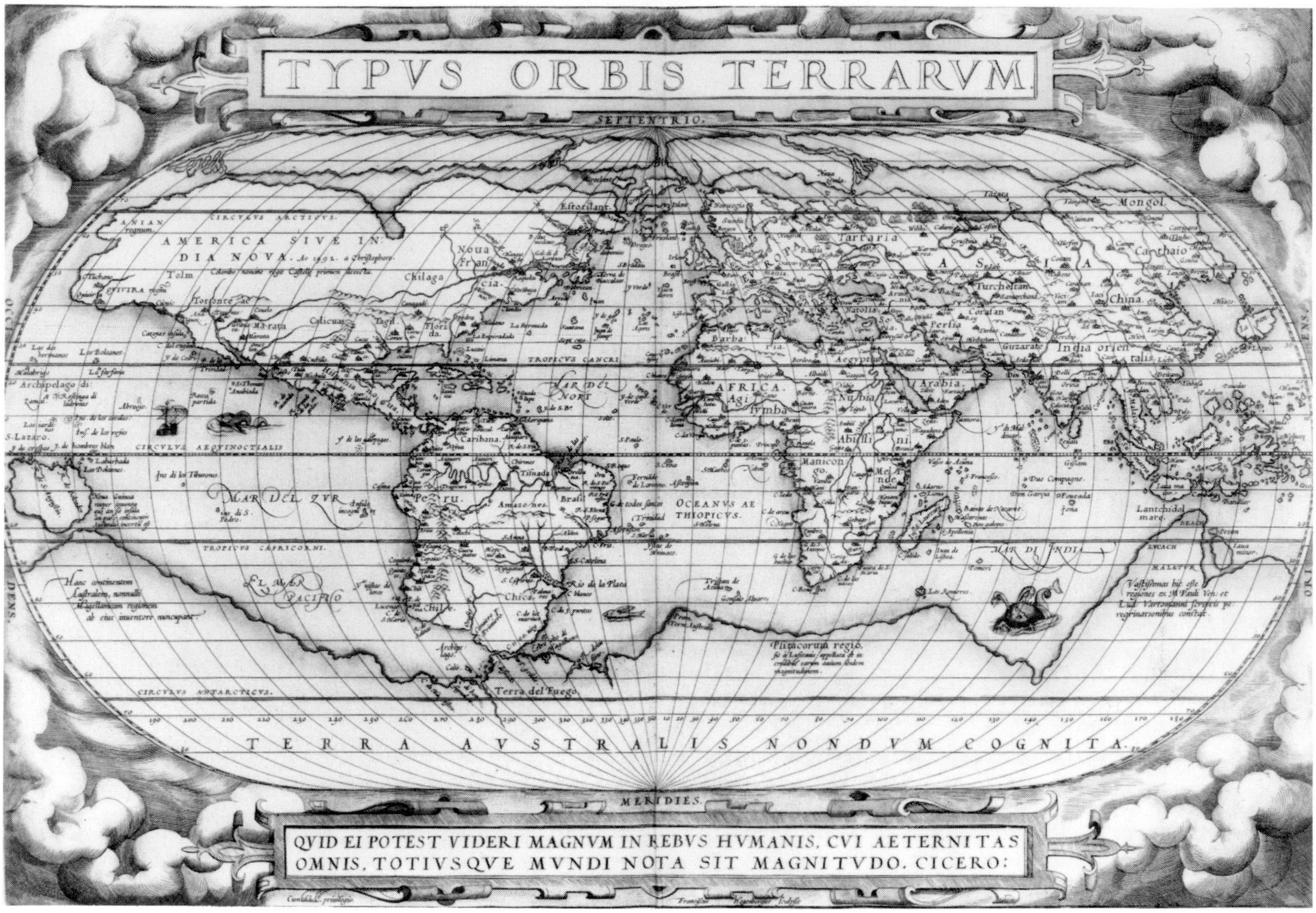

The Unknown Southern Continent covers the entire bottom of this map, first published in 1570.

lowing imagination to run riot, some writers depicted a perfect paradise, where gems and jewels were abundant, where fruits and other foods were plentiful.

When King George III of England was having trouble with his rebellious American colonies during the 1760s, advisers assured him that richer settlements could flourish on a new, still-to-be-discovered continent. The time was ripe for a worldwide British empire, whose expanded territory would increase trade and make up for the possible loss of North American territories. The Admiralty was anxious to send an able navigator into unexplored waters as quickly as possible—before the French or Spanish beat them to it. A "British Columbus" could sail into the great unknown and discover and claim an entire continent for England.

Alexander Dalrymple expected to be that Columbus. He was a prominent geographer and astronomer, and a distinguished member of the Royal Society, which consisted of England's most esteemed scientists. Dalrymple had charted seas and their currents, and he devised maps that were based on his own theories, *not* on facts. His *Account of the Discoveries made in the South Pacific Ocean Previous to 1764* described a "Great South Land"—a continent 5,323 miles wide. He assured readers that the American colonies—with their population of 2 million—were unimportant compared to the Great South Land, which was probably inhabited by 50 million people. It was so rich that "the scraps from this table would be sufficient to maintain the power, dominion, and sovereignty of Britain by employing all its manufacturers and ships."[2]

Alexander Dalrymple

The Unknown Southern Continent was a captivating goal. And there was a celestial reason for launching a major expedition. On June 3, 1769, a transit of Venus would take place: The planet Venus would pass between the earth and the sun. An accurate observation of this occurrence would enable astronomers to calculate the earth's distance from the sun. France, Spain, Russia, and Sweden were among the European countries sending 150 scientists to various parts of the world. They would be sky gazing from places as far apart as Norway, Siberia, Hudson Bay, California, and Peking. Studying the event was crucial, because another transit of Venus would not take place for 105 years—not until 1874.

Britain's Royal Society decided that the best place for viewing Venus in 1769 was the South Pacific, but it had no money and no ships for this risky, expensive project. In 1768, therefore, the Society asked His Majesty the King for help. Fortunately, George III was easily persuaded. Astronomers could study heaven's mysteries while an able navigator might discover new lands that would expand England's power. The king allotted £4,000 for an expedition and ordered the Admiralty to supply a ship, captain, and crew.

Dalrymple was confident that he would be chosen to head an expedition that would find the Great South Land. The Royal Society bolstered his self-esteem, for they considered him qualified to become an outstanding explorer. Dalrymple was elated because he assumed he would be captain.

However, the appointment of Dalrymple was "totally repugnant to the rules of the navy."[3] Only an experienced officer of the British navy could qualify. Sir Edward Hawke, First Lord of the Admiralty, said he would sooner lose his right hand than make Dalrymple commander of an expedition. However, Dalrymple would be allowed to accompany the expedition as its chief astronomer. The disappointed scientist retorted that he had "no thoughts of making this voyage as a passenger nor in any other capacity than having total management of the Ship."[4]

How offended and resentful Dalrymple was when told that a "nobody" had been chosen as captain! The Admiralty had decided upon James Cook, a sailor, not a scientist; a noncommissioned officer who had never been in charge of anything larger than a coal carrier or a small schooner.

James Cook

James Cook was the son of a poor farm laborer. He had received little formal education: only a few years of elementary schooling. At eighteen, after working for a grocer and for a shopkeeper who ran a general store, he was taken on as an apprentice by John Walker, a ship owner who ran a fleet of coal carriers from Whitby, a major port on the Yorkshire coast. Between voyages Cook lived with his employer. During his spare hours he taught himself mathematics, astronomy, and navigation.

At the age of twenty-six, Cook was offered command of a ship by Walker. Instead, Cook joined the navy as an or-

Captain James Cook

dinary seaman—a puzzling decision, because he gave up a relatively easy berth when he enlisted. British sailors had to endure harsh discipline and horrible living conditions in cramped, bug-ridden quarters. Ordinary seamen usually came from the poorest families, or they were *impressed*—kidnapped by press gangs who were paid by the navy to seize and supply men. There was little promise of advancement, because officers usually came from society's upper classes.

However, Cook's abilities were so outstanding that he became a ship's master within two years. (A master, who holds the highest noncommissioned rank, is in charge of running a ship.) In 1759, during the French and Indian War, he charted the St. Lawrence River as far as Quebec. This helped General James Wolfe advance up the river and defeat the French. After that, as master of a navy schooner, he surveyed and charted the coasts of Newfoundland, Nova Scotia, and Labrador. His accurate, detailed maps and charts excited the interest of influential leaders in the Admiralty, who perceived that Cook had exceptional talent.

The Royal Society was impressed by Cook's ability as an astronomer. After he wrote a paper describing a solar eclipse that had taken place in 1766, members judged Cook to be "a good mathematician and very expert in his Business."[5]

At forty years old, an age when most naval officers had passed their peak, Cook was singled out to lead a historic expedition. The Admiralty promptly advanced him from master to first lieutenant so that he could be its commander. The Royal Society was pleased to accept this appointment.

Cook was in charge of a ship with the aristocratic name *Earl of Pembroke*. The navy renamed it *Endeavour*. The vessel was not a beautiful, graceful warship. It was squat and unattractive, a Whitby collier, the kind Cook had sailed when he worked as a coal hauler. Small, stubby, slow, but sturdy, it had ample space for storage. Since the voyage to the Pacific was expected to last at least two years, room was essential for scientific instruments, tools, live animals intended for food, other foodstuffs, arms and ammunition, and gifts to soothe the temperaments of any natives Cook might meet.

At first the destination was vague. Most of the Pacific Ocean was a mystery. Some South Sea Islands, such as the Marquesas and the Tongas, had been discovered during the sixteenth century but had then been "lost." Subsequent navigators could not find them again because they had not been properly charted.

Fortunately, before Cook left, the British explorer Samuel Wallis returned to England. He had accurately charted the geographic location of a South Sea island where fresh water was abundant, flowers and fruits grew everywhere, and beautiful native women were eager and adept at lovemaking. Wallis had found Tahiti, an island that sounded like paradise.[6] Without bothering to consult its people—a well-established explorer's habit—Wallis had claimed it for the Crown and named it King George III Island.

"Queen" Purea of Tahiti greets Captain Samuel Wallis, June 1767.

Tahiti was a fine spot for the viewing of Venus. More important, it was an ideal base for exploration, because Wallis was positive that the Unknown Southern Continent was just south of the island. His crew told him they had seen its huge mountain peaks in the distance, but because Wallis had been sick at that time, he couldn't investigate. The Royal Society recommended Tahiti for astronomical viewing. The British government approved because it hoped Cook could find a stupendous new continent nearby.

Drastic renovations were needed for the ship: cabins for Cook and his officers; a bigger deck for seamen's hammocks and for three boats that would explore shorelines and land; a larger galley for cooking; storage for extra cables and sails. Eight tons of iron were needed for ballast (weight used as a stabilizer). The *Endeavour* was a tight ship in many ways. It had to accommodate eighty-three people. There was no room to spare.

A Privileged Passenger

Imagine Cook's consternation when told he must accommodate eleven additional people. The Admiralty had delivered the following orders to him: "You are hereby requir'd & directed to receive on board . . . [the astronomer] Mr. Charles Green and his Servant & Baggage, and also the said Joseph Banks Esq. and his Suite consisting of eight Persons with their Baggage."[7]

Joseph Banks was twenty-four years old, handsome, rich, disarmingly charming, and eager to travel anywhere in the world—not only for the sake of adventure but also because he was passionately interested in botany and zoology. This extraordinary young man's inherited wealth would have allowed him to live the leisurely life of a London gentleman.

Joseph Banks, painted by Joshua Reynolds

He preferred field study in faraway places, however, and had proven his mettle by enduring Newfoundland's harsh climate in order to collect plants and animal specimens.

When Banks heard about the impending trip to the South Seas he hungered to go along and offered to pay for the privilege. His friend Lord Sandwich used his influence to grant Banks's wish. Young, rich Mr. Banks paid for his group's passage: £10,000, an enormous sum at that time. The

Royal Society endorsed Banks, who was one of its members. The Society approved, not because he was a great scientist, but because he was "a gentleman of Large Fortune well versed in Natural History."[8]

Cook made room for Banks, Banks's four servants, two naturalists, Daniel Solander and Herman Sporing, and two artists, Sydney Parkinson and Alexander Buchan. He moved officers into cramped spaces below deck so that Banks and his artists and scientists could have well-ventilated, reasonably spacious private cabins. Additional mounds of baggage and equipment were taken aboard. There was Banks's library of natural history books; his "machines" for catching and preserving insects; his nets, drags, and hooks for fish; materials for preserving animals and plants; artists' equipment; and space for his two pet greyhounds.

Official Instructions

Detailed instructions were issued by the Admiralty. Cook was to proceed southward "in order to make discovery of the Continent" mentioned by Wallis, where he was expected to describe the people and "endeavour by all proper means to cultivate the Friendship and Alliance with the natives . . . Shewing them every kind of Civility and Regard."[9] All newly found lands, even those that were uninhabited, were to be charted and claimed in the name of the king. ("Claiming" usually entailed planting the British flag or leaving a note on a tree or stone indicating the date and nationality of the discoverer.)

In addition to official orders from the Admiralty, Cook received a set of instructions called *Hints* from the Earl of Morton, president of the Royal Society. Emphasizing that "the primary object of the Expedition is to take a correct observation of the Transit of Venus," Morton wrote about encountering people on the Unknown Southern Continent. Assuming that, because of its size, it was probably occupied by a "most civilized" nation, he advised respect, restraint, and humane behavior. Morton asked for detailed descriptions of the inhabitants' "progress in Arts or Science" and information about their language, religion, morals, and government.[10]

Captain Cook was embarking upon the eighteenth century's version of a space voyage. Lord Morton speculated that the captain might discover terrestrials who were more highly civilized than Europeans.

1768-1771

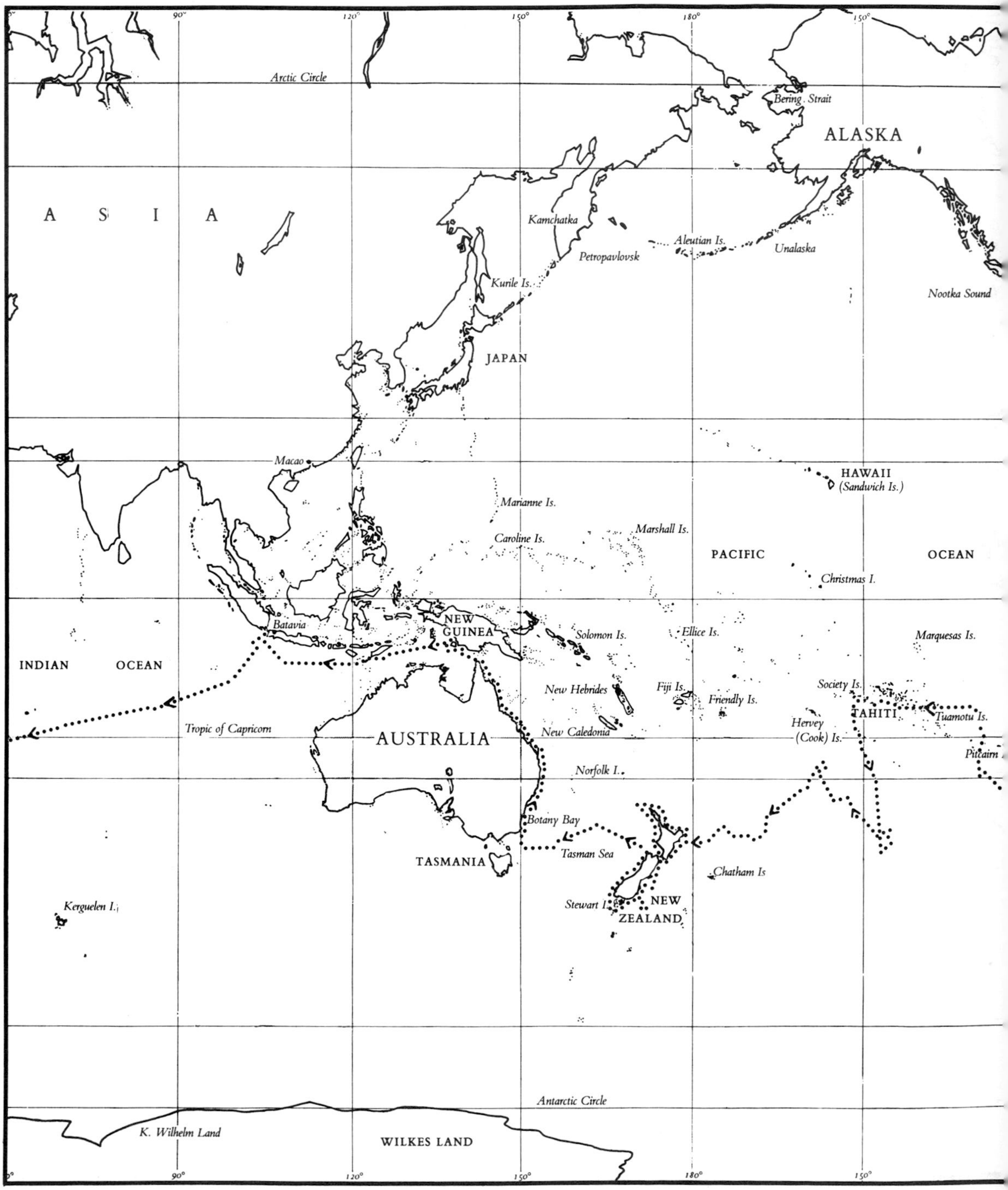
90°
120°
150°
180°
150°
Arctic Circle
Bering Strait
ALASKA
A S I A
Kamchatka
Aleutian Is.
Petropavlovsk
Unalaska
Kurile Is.
Nootka Sound
JAPAN
Macao
HAWAII
(Sandwich Is.)
Marianne Is.
Marshall Is.
Caroline Is.
PACIFIC
OCEAN
Christmas I.
NEW
GUINEA
Batavia
Solomon Is.
Ellice Is.
Marquesas Is.
INDIAN
OCEAN
New Hebrides
Fiji Is.
Friendly Is.
Society Is.
TAHITI
Tuamotu Is.
Hervey
(Cook) Is.
Pitcairn
Tropic of Capricorn
AUSTRALIA
New Caledonia
Norfolk I.
Botany Bay
Tasman Sea
TASMANIA
Chatham Is
Stewart I.
NEW
ZEALAND
Kerguelen I.
Antarctic Circle
K. Wilhelm Land
WILKES LAND
90°
120°
150°
180°
150°

The First Voyage

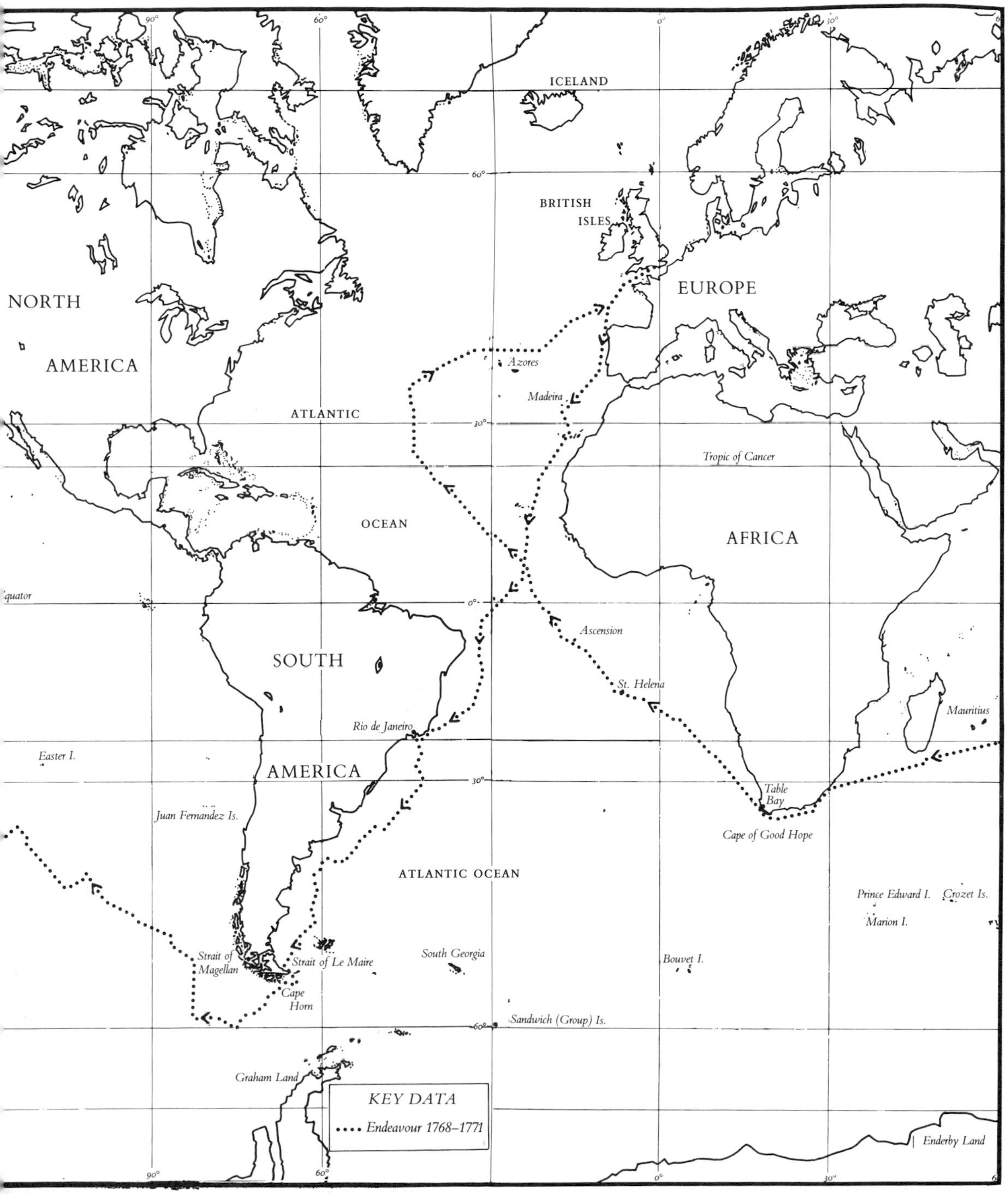

ICELAND
BRITISH
ISLES
EUROPE
NORTH
AMERICA
Azores
Madeira
ATLANTIC
OCEAN
Tropic of Cancer
AFRICA
quator
Ascension
SOUTH
AMERICA
St. Helena
Mauritius
Rio de Janeiro
Easter I.
Table
Bay
Juan Fernandez Is.
Cape of Good Hope
ATLANTIC OCEAN
Prince Edward I.
Crozet Is.
Marion I.
Strait of
Magellan
Strait of Le Maire
South Georgia
Bouvet I.
Cape
Horn
Sandwich (Group) Is.
Graham Land
KEY DATA
Endeavour 1768–1771
Enderby Land

The *Endeavour* leaving England, August 1768

2 · VOYAGE TO TAHITI

ON AUGUST 26, 1768, the *Endeavour* set sail from Plymouth, England. Three weeks later the ship docked at the island of Madeira for onions, fruit, beef, a live bull (for future meals), water, and 3,032 gallons of wine. Wine was an important beverage because fresh water became stale, smelly, and repulsive after staying in casks for some time. Since liquid was vital, wine, rum, and beer were carried in quantity.

Life at sea could prove so monotonous that any excuse for celebration was welcome. Crossing the equator was an occasion for fun. "Every one that could not prove upon a Sea Chart that he had before crossed the Line, was either to pay a bottle of Rum or be ducked in the sea."[1] The crew submitted a list of eligible victims that even included dogs and cats. Twenty-two men preferred ducking to giving up a ration of rum. Banks paid in brandy so that he, his servants, and his dogs wouldn't be plunged overboard in a chair rigged up for the occasion.

In November the expedition stopped at Rio de Janeiro, Brazil, a Portuguese port that usually welcomed ships needing provisions. However, the country's viceroy, His Excellency Count Rolim, was suspicious. He was positive the

Endeavour was not part of the British Royal Navy because it wasn't an impressive battleship, and so he ordered Brazilian soldiers to keep watch by rowing around the anchored *Endeavour*.

Cook was incensed because he needed permission to go ashore and talk to the viceroy. When he was eventually allowed to see Count Rolim, Cook was guarded by a Brazilian soldier, and one of the ship's officers was held hostage until his meeting had ended.

When Cook explained the purpose of the expedition the viceroy's suspicions increased. What sane captain would sail halfway across the world to look at a star called Venus? His Excellency was positive he was dealing with spies, especially after Cook asked if Banks could be allowed on shore in order to collect plants. Rolim was certain that Banks was more interested in fortifications than flowers, and he therefore refused permission.

Determined to "botanize" in South America, Joseph Banks managed to sneak into the countryside. After bribing soldiers who were guarding the ship, he and one of his assistants slipped out of a cabin window in the middle of the night. Using a rope, they lowered themselves into a boat, rowed to shore, hastily collected plants and shrubs, then brought their precious greens back to the *Endeavour*. They were elated because they had found many species new to science.[2]

Cook had to tolerate the rules set down by the viceroy because he needed supplies. His men were allowed to buy provisions, but they were guarded by Brazilian soldiers whenever they made purchases and whenever they loaded cargo. He protested but was helpless when some of his men were arrested and thrown into a dank dungeon overnight because they had not been accompanied by a soldier.

Cook was anxious to get away from a country in which he and his men were under guard, but he couldn't leave because of contrary winds and severe storms. He had to stay

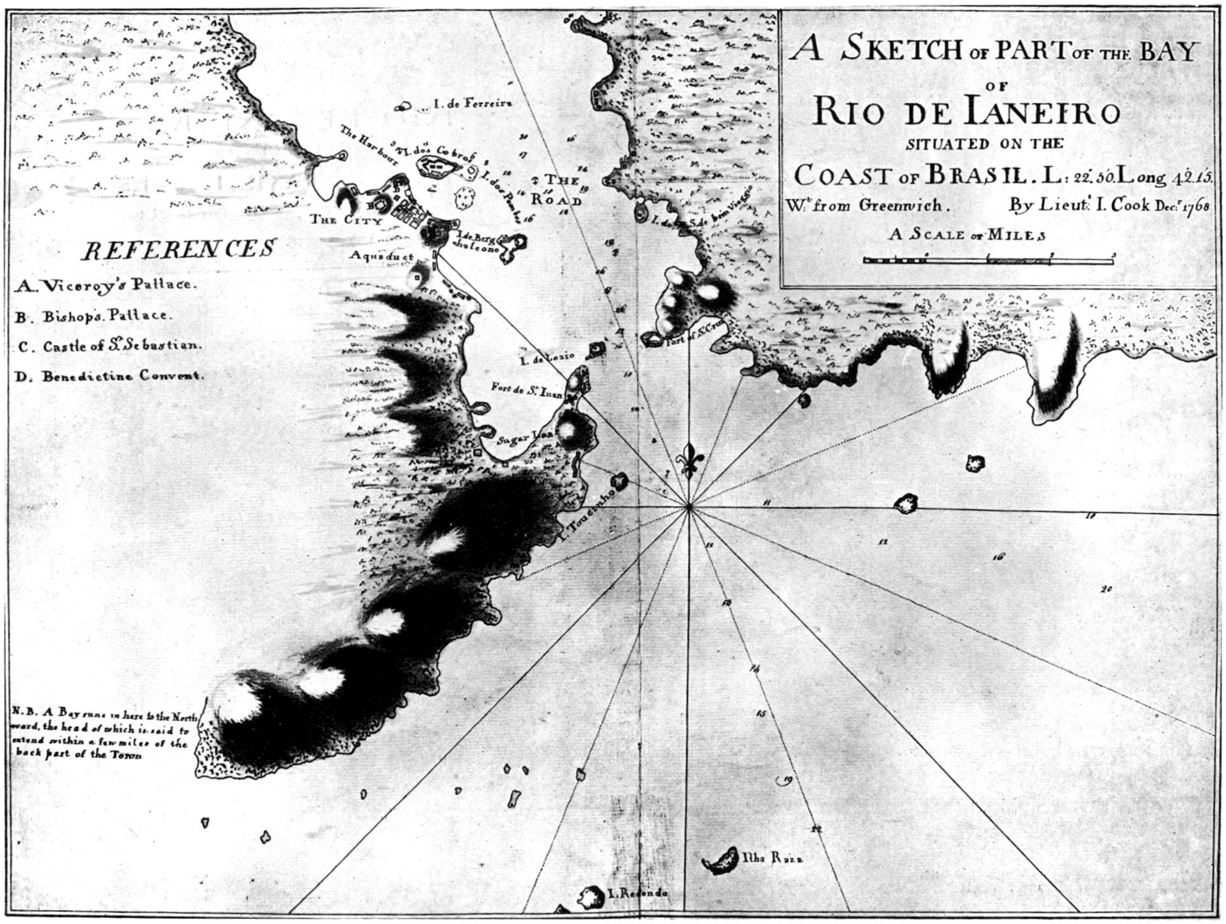

Cook's sketch of Rio de Janeiro

for twenty-six days. During that time he charted Rio de Janeiro's harbor and sketched its fortifications—had the viceroy known, the *Endeavour* would have surely been attacked as a spy ship.

Land of Giants

On January 16, 1769, the expedition arrived at Tierra del Fuego, on the southern tip of South America. This land was also called Patagonia, a word meaning "big feet." It was reputedly the home of giants who were at least twelve feet tall. In 1764, only four years before Cook set sail on the *Endeavour*, the British captain John Byron declared he had

The *Endeavour* crew at a watering place near Cape Horn

met a Patagonian chief of "gigantic stature" and referred to the natives as "monsters in a human shape."[3] Dalrymple's writings repeated the legend as fact, and the Royal Society believed that Patagonian giants probably existed. Newspapers printed sensational "factual" accounts about frightful, fascinating human hulks. According to one version, an English sailor's head barely reached a Patagonian's hips.

Some members of the *Endeavour* expedition were disappointed because they didn't meet giants. Banks measured the natives, "their height being from five feet eight inches to five feet ten inches . . . the women . . . seldom exceeding five feet."[4]

Cook felt sorry for the plight of these average-size "Indians."[5] He thought them "perhaps as miserable a set of People as are this day upon Earth."[6] Men and women scantily clothed in seal or guanaco skins lived with their children in open huts that looked like large beehives. (Had these natives visited London's slums they would have been shocked to see hungry people dressed in rags, living in filthy hovels.)

While Cook kept his men busy getting wood and water for the ship, Banks hunted for plants. He organized a party consisting of his two artists, his four servants, two sailors, the astronomer Green, and the ship's surgeon, Monkhouse. A sudden snowstorm kept them from returning to the ship for the night. By morning two of Banks's servants had frozen to death. Freezing, exhausted, heartsick, and hungry, the survivors made their way back to the *Endeavour*.

Rounding Cape Horn, which is the southern tip of South America, was the next challenge. Its rough waters and terrifying storms had wrecked countless ships. The voyage between the Atlantic and Pacific oceans could take months because of horrendous waves and furious gales. Fortunately, unusually good weather enabled them to round the Cape in thirty-three days. Occasionally the sea was calm enough for Banks to go boating and shoot seabirds for his collection. After measuring wingspans and examining bone structures, these usually ended up in the cooking pot. Banks declared albatross delicious—when cooked with a delectable sauce.

A Patagonian family

Cook had access to Dalrymple's charts and notes.[7] When the *Endeavour* reached the Pacific Ocean, it plowed southwest through waters in the very area that Dalrymple had drawn as part of the Unknown Southern Continent. It was disappointing, especially for Banks, who had eagerly anticipated finding a fabulous land.

Cook, on the other hand, was skeptical. He gave up his search for a continent in southern waters and steered his ship northwest. "I do not think myself at liberty to spend time in searching for what I was sure not to find," he wrote in his *Journals*.[8]

On April 13, 1769, nine months after having left England, the *Endeavour* anchored in Matavai Bay, Tahiti.

3 · PACIFIC PARADISE

TAHITI, extolled as a magnificent tropical island with abundant food and affectionate people! Some of the *Endeavour*'s men had been on the *Dolphin* with Captain Wallis when he discovered Tahiti two years before. They had succumbed to the embraces of irresistible native women, who had become so attached to their British visitors that they had actually wept when the *Dolphin* sailed away. The crew anticipated a perfect paradise.

Lieutenant Gore was an American from Virginia who had been with the Wallis expedition. Upon landing at Matavai

Matavai Bay, Tahiti

Bay, he reported to Cook "that a very great revolution must have happen'd."[1] The lovely huts he remembered had been destroyed, and he couldn't find many of his native friends. He did not know, and probably could not conceive, that tribal wars took place in this sailors' Garden of Eden. Just a few months before Cook's arrival, Tahitians from another part of the island had attacked the people of this area.[2]

However, newcomers who had never seen the island were not disillusioned. Tahitians offered green boughs as tokens of peace. Then, they showed off nature's bounty, consisting of vast groves of banana plants and coconut and breadfruit trees. Favorable climate and fertile soil freed natives from back-breaking labor.

Banks was ecstatic. He described the land as "the truest picture of an arcadia [an ideal country] . . . of which we were going to be kings."[3] Cook's reaction was more reserved. Although duly impressed by the lushness of the land and the beauty, grace, and cleanliness of the people (they bathed at least three times a day), he was annoyed by the natives' penchant for "stealing every thing that came within their reach."[4] The second day on shore two men had "their pockets pick'd the one of his spy glass and the other of his snuff Box."[5] The next day a more serious incident occurred. A Tahitian grabbed a sentry's gun. The officer in charge gave orders to fire, and the native was shot dead. Cook had been away hunting with Banks when this took place. Upon returning he explained to the islanders "that the man was kill'd for taking away the Musquet," but despite this he and his men "would still would be friends with them."[6]

Tahitians did not share Europeans' belief in the sanctity of private property. They were constantly tempted by items they had never seen before. Like collectors impelled to acquire unusual objects, they took things that looked interesting, even though they had no use for them. Taking objects on the sly required skill. One clever fellow managed to snatch

Breadfruit

Cook's stockings from under his head while he was lying awake in bed. Banks, who dressed elegantly "even in the wilderness," was sad to discover that his beautiful silver-trimmed white jacket and waistcoat had been taken.[7]

Losses of this sort were of little consequence, but the taking of a quadrant caused quite a commotion. The quadrant was an invaluable, irreplaceable tool essential for navigation and for observing the transit of Venus. Astonished that a heavy object of this sort could be carried away despite guards, and agitated because of the loss, Cook immediately seized all the large canoes that were offshore and didn't release them until the quadrant was returned hours later.

The islanders' penchant for taking things was so exasperating that when an iron rake was missing, Cook detained twenty-five large canoes that were loaded with fish and had them moored close to his encampment. Even after the rake was returned he kept the canoes, hoping that muskets, pistols, and other pilfered items would be brought back. After three days, however, the fish began to rot and stink. Cook surrendered, glad to have the canoes paddled away.

Fort Venus

Cook chose a site on the beach for observing the transit. Tents were set up to accommodate about forty-five men, including Cook, his officers, and Banks's party. There was an observatory, a kitchen, and work space for the ship's carpenters and sailmakers. The camp, called Fort Venus, was completed in two weeks. Surrounded by a wall that had six swivel guns, it was constantly guarded by sentinels. Cook remarked that he felt "perfectly secure from any thing these people [the Tahitians] could attempt."[8]

Fort Venus was off limits to all island natives, except for specially invited guests. Purea, touted by Wallis as "Queen of the Island" was always welcome. Cook was delighted to see her, for he presumed she ruled Tahiti. He was applying European conceptions about government: that kings or queens reigned supreme in every land. But there were no kings or queens here. The land was divided among chiefs, and Purea was the daughter of a chief.

Banks praised Tahiti as an island "where Love is the Cheif Occupation, the favourite, nay almost the Sole Luxury of the inhabitants; both the bodies and souls of the women are moulded into the utmost perfection."[9] He concluded that although European women had better complexions, in all other ways native women were "superior."[10] Banks chose Tiatia, who was one of Purea's handmaidens, as his ladylove and referred to her as "my flame."

Some of the girls insisted upon gifts. During Wallis's visit the price for lovemaking had been nails. Sailors had extracted them from the *Dolphin*'s planks. They even pulled out nails that held up their hammocks, so that many of them had to sleep on the floor. Knowing this, it is no surprise that Cook sentenced a sailor who was caught stealing nails to two dozen lashes.[11]

On June 3, the date of the transit, there was not a cloud in the sky. It seemed perfect for observing the planet Venus. In addition to scientists at the fort, Cook sent observers to the west and to the east with instructions about describing the outerspace event. Unfortunately, a penumbra (a hazy glow surrounding the planet) spoiled the viewing, so that the observations were a failure, not only for this expedition but for others all over the world.

Astonishing Customs

Fortunately, there were other observations that were to have a tremendous impression upon Europeans: new knowledge about Pacific islanders, whose life-style of ease and plenty seemed enviable and whose practices proved fascinating.

Banks was a perfect observer, willingly participating in rites and rituals, astutely describing costumes and customs on this "Island of Sensuality."[12] In his opinion, Tahitian clothing was more natural and graceful than the elaborate dresses and suits worn by Europeans. Tahitian women reminded him of artists' "goddesses and angels in loose folds of Cloth not shaped to their bodies exactly."[13]

Banks remarked about the huge appetites of the natives, noting that one man ate a meal consisting of "3 bread fruits each bigger than two fists, 2 or 3 fish and 14 or 15 plantains [similar to bananas] . . . and concluded his dinner with about a quart of a food as substancial as the thickest unbaked custard." This was not unusual, Banks wrote, because "plumpness . . . is valued as beauty."[14]

Girls' bodies were decorated with tattoos that covered their buttocks and thighs. Banks watched a tattooing performed on a twelve-year-old girl, who suffered from hundreds of pricks that drew blood. The procedure lasted at least one hour, and it was so excruciatingly painful that two women had to hold the girl down. Banks was so interested in having a permanent skin design on his own body that he had his arm tattooed. Banks had started a sailors' tradition.

This young sophisticated gentleman from England volunteered to participate in native ceremonies. He played a dramatic role during a funeral. Stripped, wearing a small cloth around his waist like the other participants, Banks was "smutted from head to foot" with charcoal and water.[15] After running about with the mourners, he joined them by plunging into a river, where they scrubbed each other clean. The purpose, according to Banks, was to look frightful and mad with grief, then wash off the symbolic dirt-coat of sorrow. When women in mourning gashed the tops of their heads using sharks' teeth until blood flowed freely, Banks was so moved that he held one of them in his arms until her bleeding stopped.

Cook was also intrigued by strange customs. Like Banks, he relished adventure and was fascinated by different cultures. Cook's *Journals* are rich with observations about Tahitians. For example:

—An important chief was carried on another's shoulders so that his feet would never touch the ground.

—An important chief could never help himself to food but had to be fed by his attendants. "There were always some Women present . . . [to] put the Victuals into his mouth."[16]

—Roasted dog was a favorite food. (At first Cook was

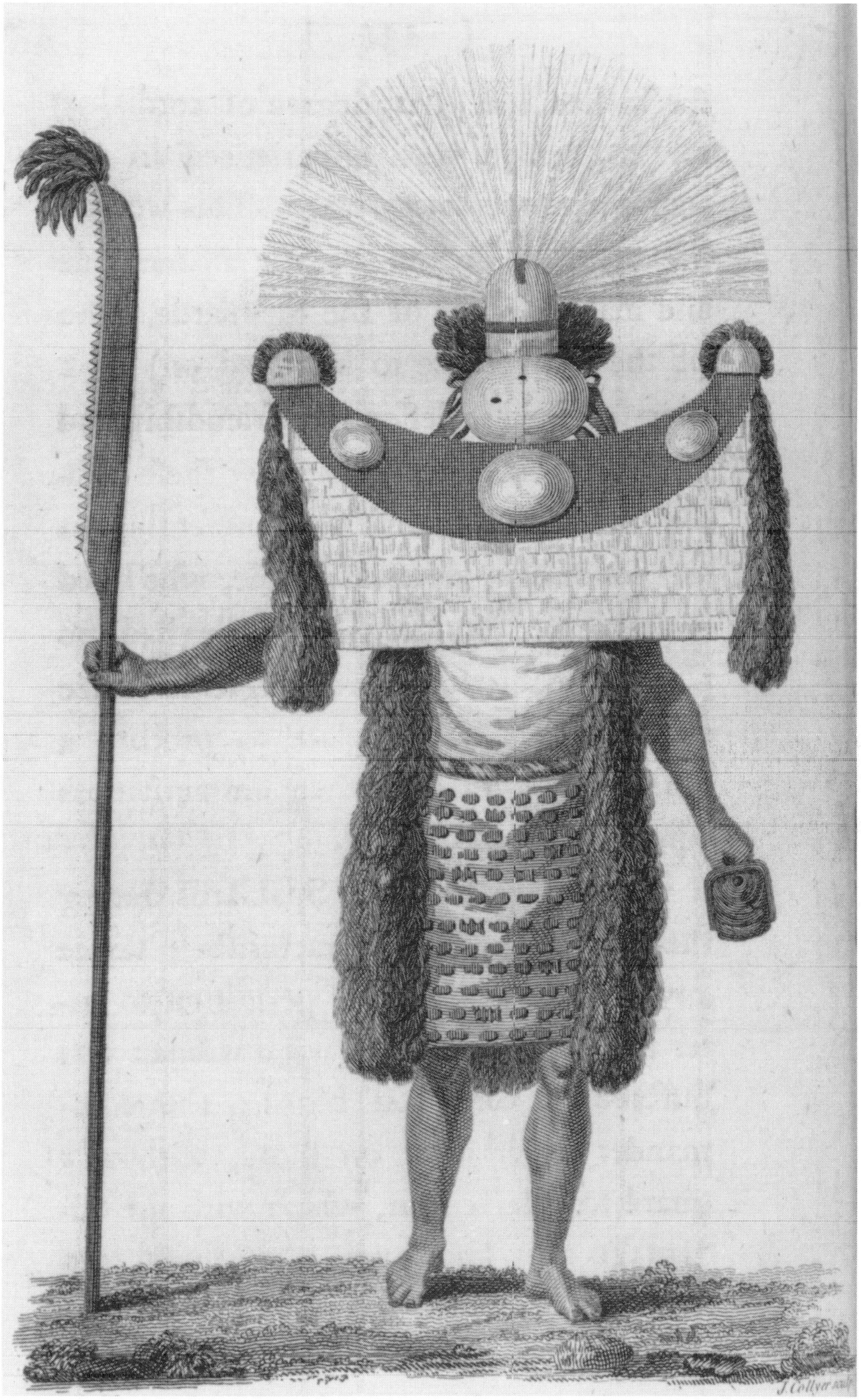

A Tahitian in mourning dress

reluctant to eat dog, but he was either too curious or too polite to refuse. He decided that he had never eaten sweeter meat.)

—Women were never permitted to eat with men. When natives were told that in England men and women ate together, they expressed disgust. However, Cook noted that "when a woman was alone in our company she would eat with us but always took [care] that her country people should not know."[17]

—"Young girls when ever they can collect 8 or 10 together dance a very indecent dance . . . singing most indecent songs and useing most indecent action in the practice of which they are brought up from their earlyest Childhood."[18]

—Tahitian musicians beat sharkskin drums and played flutes, which "they blow with one nostril stoping the other with the thum of the left hand."[19]

Like Banks, Cook made detailed notes about Tahitians'

A double canoe and a boathouse

A priest of the Society Islands

tools, weapons, carvings, and their methods of fishing, building canoes, and making cloth. He described their houses and their many stone-paved temples, called *maraes*. At first Cook thought these were burial grounds, then later realized that they were places of worship. It was unfortunate that some of the *Endeavour*'s men pulled stones from a *marae* to be used as extra ballast for the ship. They had to be stopped by islanders who were outraged to see their sacred ground despoiled.

It was hard for Cook and Banks to believe that on this island of paradise, priests often smothered their own new-born children. On the other hand, Tahitians would have been horrified had they known that in Britain an eight-year-old child could be hanged for stealing something worth a few pennies. Tahitians were even upset by floggings. They would have been appalled by jails, debtors' prisons, and insane asylums; horrified by the filth, poverty, and crime in England at that time.

Compared with conditions in England or confinement on ship, Tahiti seemed to be an ideal escape. Just before the *Endeavour* was ready to sail away, two men deserted. This was a serious matter, for all hands were needed. Cook chose a deplorable way of forcing their return. He seized hostages. Purea and six chiefs were held captive until the deserters, Clement Webb and Sam Gibson, were found and brought to the ship. These men confessed that they had become so strongly attached to two native girls that they couldn't bear to leave. Webb and Gibson were confined to quarters until the ship sailed. They received two dozen lashes each as punishment.

Although Tahiti was a paradise for the *Endeavour*'s crew, quite a few Tahitians wanted to leave it and sail to England. Only two islanders were allowed to join the expedition: Chief Tupia and his boy servant, Tayeto. Cook wanted Tupia on board because he was a skilled navigator who could guide him to other Pacific islands.

Banks was enthralled at the prospect of introducing a Pacific island chief to society. "I do not know why I may not keep him as a curiosity, as well as some of my neighbours do lions and tygers at a larger expence than he will probably ever put to me," he quipped, noting "the amusement I shall have in his future conversation, and the benefit he [Tupia] will be of to this ship . . . will I think fully repay me."[20]

Before leaving, Cook charted the Tahitian coast in detail and made many inland excursions. July 13, 1769, Cook sailed away. He hoisted a British flag and took possession of the nearby islands, which he named the Society Islands, "as they lay contiguous [near] to one another."[21] He then sailed southwest, in quest of his most important objective: finding the Southern Continent not yet discovered.

A Tahitian mother and child

4 · CANNIBALS AND GOBLINS

THEY SAILED through a seemingly endless seascape where (according to Dalrymple) there was supposed to be land. Everyone, including Cook, was disappointed. The *Endeavour* was at sea for two months before the twelve-year-old ship's boy, Nicholas Young, sighted land. He received a gallon of rum as a reward.

Cook had arrived at New Zealand, a country that had been discovered by the Dutch navigator Abel Tasman in 1642. Tasman never disembarked, because alarmed natives had clubbed and killed four of his men who were rowing toward shore in one of the ship's small boats. Tasman was sure New Zealand was the "unexplored Southern Continent."

Cook hoped that Tasman was right. Everyone was exhilarated. Banks wrote, "All hands seem to agree that this is certainly the Continent we are in search of."[1] The *Endeavour*'s men were the first Europeans to land in New Zealand.

Not only did Europeans discover New Zealanders; New Zealanders discovered Europeans, and we know their reactions from their oral history. They were terrified when they first saw the *Endeavour*. The ship seemed to be a monstrous, supernatural water bird. Its occupants were goblins with eyes in the backs of their heads—for how else could they head

A New Zealand war canoe

toward shore going (rowing) backward? The goblins owned "thunder sticks" that flashed lightning and killed when aimed at any living creature. Some of these aliens collected shells, flowers, tree blossoms, and stones, probably for magical reasons. Luckily the goblins were good, giving food and gifts, and "the great lord" James Cook was their kind, gentle leader, who patted their children's heads.[2]

The *Endeavour*'s arrival with strange-looking aliens was indeed a calamity at first. When New Zealanders suddenly appeared from the woods, seamen opened fire and killed one person. And when a canoe crammed with armed warriors tried to attack the *Endeavour*, English guns killed four more. Three who dived into the sea to escape gunshot were picked

[redacted]

Maoris defying their enemies

up and brought on board. The youngest of these rescued warriors may have been only ten years old. Surprised that they weren't harmed but were treated kindly, these boys were glad to be on the *Endeavour*—especially because they feared a rival tribe might kill them. When the boys were put ashore they hid in the bushes for self-protection.

The sight from the ship of hundreds of warriors armed with heavy bludgeons for skull-splitting was reason enough to leave this area. Cook called it Poverty Bay, "because it afforded us no one thing we wanted."[3] Before leaving Cook raised the Union Jack and claimed the land in the name of His Majesty King George III.

As the *Endeavour* cruised along the coastline, Cook saw huge, elaborately carved canoes crowded with warriors, who tried to frighten his men by shaking their lances and clubs.

They shouted and stuck out their tongues as signs of defiance. However, Cook also encountered friendly tribes during numerous land excursions.

Cook was astounded that Tupia could understand the inhabitants, who identified themselves as Maoris. Tupia's Tahitian home was two thousand miles away, yet he could communicate, because the Maoris spoke a Polynesian dialect. The captain found it mind-boggling that Pacific islanders must have navigated great distances without compasses and quadrants.[4]

While Cook was primarily concerned with geography, Banks was elated not only by the many new specimens of plants he collected but also by his encounters with people never seen before by western man. He was disappointed that Maori women didn't seem as enticing as Tahitian girls. Their hair was daubed with fish or bird fat. Their lips were tattooed black. Large holes in their earlobes were packed with cloth, feathers, bones, sticks, and fingernails or teeth of dead relatives. Banks complained that "the women were plain and made themselves more so by painting their faces with red ocre and oil which generally was fresh and wet upon cheeks and foreheads, easily transferrable to the noses of anyone who should attempt to kiss them. . . . The noses of several of our people evidently shewd [showed]." Nevertheless Banks praised them "as great coquetts [flirts] as any Europeans could be."[5]

Men's faces had swirls of tattoos. No two designs were alike. Nose holes enabled males to enhance their makeup. Sticks, and sometimes feathers, pierced their nostrils and spread across their cheeks.

Finding out that the Maoris were cannibals who ate their enemies was a terrible shock. Several came on board to demonstrate in front of the *Endeavour*'s men that this was common practice. They gnawed a human bone "in such a manner as plainly shew'd that the flesh was to them a dainty bit."[6]

Otegoongoon, the son of a New Zealand chief

Although the English probably believed that cannibalism was motivated by hate or hunger, this was not so. Enemies' bodies were eaten to absorb the courage, spirit, and strength of the deceased.

Banks discovered baskets of human bones. Using Tupia as an interpreter, he learned that these were the remains of seven enemies. Skulls with the flesh preserved on them were kept as trophies. Banks managed to buy one. He paid for it with "a pair of old Drawers of very white linnen."[7] Cook also bought a souvenir: the bone of a forearm "half pick'd to Convince the World that there are Cannibals."[8]

After six months and 2,400 miles of brilliant navigation and charting, Cook realized that New Zealand was not that long-sought-after continent but two large islands. He believed the land was ideal for a British colony because the soil was fertile, its timber was excellent, and the waters teemed with fish.

Maoris challenging Cook's men to fight

An English officer bartering with a Maori

His accomplishment was momentous. He had found a land the size of Britain, which he viewed as promising for colonists who could raise European crops and enjoy prosperity. And despite the first few skirmishes and their cannibalism, Cook judged the Maoris to be friendly and intelligent.

On April 1, 1770, the *Endeavour* sailed from New Zealand. Cook would have liked to return to England by way of Cape Horn to find out whether a continent existed in that direction, but the onset of the southern winter made this impossible. Therefore, hoping to investigate new territory, he headed west toward Australia.

5 · A UNIQUE LAND

TWO WEEKS AFTER leaving New Zealand the *Endeavour* reached Australia, then called New Holland. It had been discovered in 1606 by Willem Jansz, a Dutch navigator who had landed on its northern shores. During the seventeenth century other Dutch explorers navigating along the north, east, and western coasts had decided that New Holland was worthless for trade; it was not even useful as a stopover because it couldn't supply provisions. William Dampier, a British buccaneer, reached the north coast of New Holland in 1686 but found nothing to plunder, and he judged its natives "the miserablest People in the world."[1]

Cook was determined to investigate a land that had been disregarded for nearly a century. Until the *Endeavour* arrived, no European had ever seen the eastern part of this vast continent.

When the English disembarked the natives ran away, except for two men who were resolved to oppose them. This brave pair threatened the *Endeavour*'s party with long spears. They retreated only after musket fire had wounded one of them.

Australian aborigines did not resemble Tahitians nor New Zealanders. They were shorter and darker. They wore no clothing and decorated their bodies with white and red paint. Tupia could not understand their language. Because they looked different he was so prejudiced that he called them *Taata Eno's*, meaning "evil people."[2]

Cook, on the other hand, described them as attractive, timid, and "inoffensive."[3] He was puzzled by their lack of interest in clothes, combs, beads, nails, mirrors, and other gifts. They had no desire for possessions. Cook noted that they refused such gifts: "They had not so much as touch'd the things we had left in their hutts. . . . All they seem'd to want was for us to be gone."[4]

The Australian aborigines found no reason for covering their bodies with cloth. One of them used a shirt as a head-

Two men who opposed Cook's landing

dress, but most gifts of clothing weren't used. They were discarded and piled in heaps as useless. Nudity was natural; clothing was senseless. Shirts and pants were such a great mystery that natives asked some sailors to strip in order to see whether these alien intruders were built like normal men.

Banks judged them to be "but one degree from Brutes," yet he envied their lack of desire for material things that Europeans found necessary.[5] Cook was also impressed by their disregard for gifts. He wrote, "In reality they are far happier than we Europeans. . . . They live in Tranquillity. . . . The Earth and sea of their own accord furnishes them with all things necessary for life."[6]

Natives didn't want foreigners' possessions, so there was no problem with "thievery." However, Banks applied a different standard of honesty for himself. He "thought it no improper measure" to take forty or fifty lances that he found in houses while their owners were away. He merely wanted the spears for his South Seas collection.[7]

Banks was delighted by the bewildering varieties of grasses, shrubs, and trees. Cook joined Banks on some of his nature walks and caught his infectious enthusiasm for "botanizing." It inspired him to name the harbor Botany Bay. Although the natives did not cultivate the soil, Cook and Banks concluded that the ground was so fertile that European crops could flourish in this unique land—an opinion that later influenced the government to choose Australia as a colony.[8]

Trapped on a Reef

On May 6, 1770, the *Endeavour* left Botany Bay. Navigating close to shore so that Cook could chart the coastline, the ship threaded its way through treacherous shoals. After weeks of dangerous sailing, a hidden reef punctured the ship's hull. The *Endeavour* was stuck fast, trapped in the Great Barrier Reef, the largest maze of coral reefs in the world. So much water gushed in that all pumps were needed to keep it afloat. Twenty miles from shore, shipwreck seemed certain! "The fear of Death now stard [stared] us in the face," Banks wrote.[9]

The men threw tons of ballast overboard, as well as cannon, guns, tools, and firewood. They were trying to lighten the ship so that it might float free of the reef. Cook sent out boats, hoping rowers with ropes could pull the *Endeavour* off the reef. The ship didn't budge, and water poured into its punctured hull. Banks admired the calm of sailors who worked the pumps nonstop for thirty-six hours. Fortunately, a high tide lifted and freed the *Endeavour* from the coral. Then the men *fothered* the bottom: A mixture of rope fibers, wool, and dung (from live sheep kept aboard) was spread on a sail. The sail was hauled under the ship's bottom by ropes to cover the leaking hole.

Cook's damaged ship, on the Endeavour River

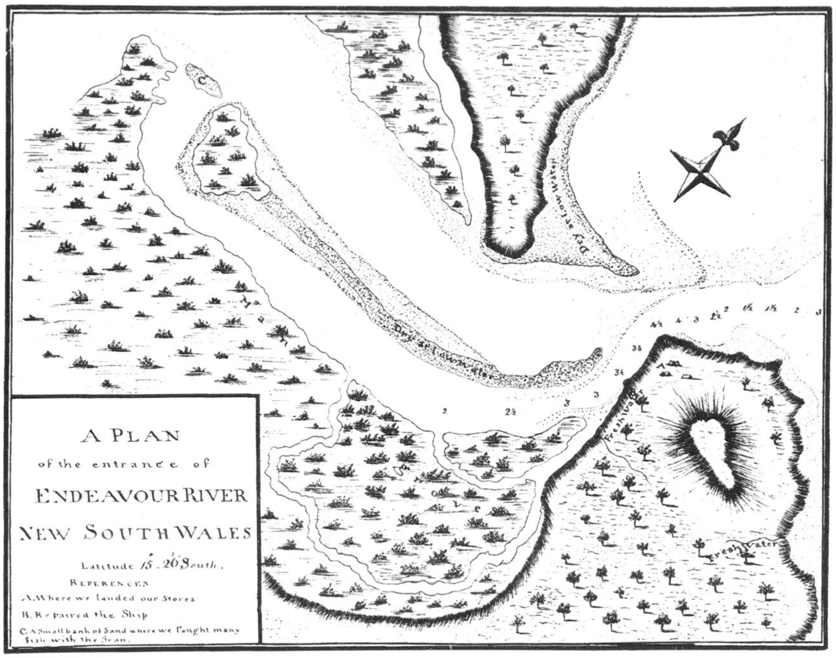

Cook's sketch of the Endeavour River

Finding a place to land was a nightmare because the sea was studded with shoals. After two harrowing days, Cook found a safe harbor. When the crew hauled their ship onto the beach for repairs, they saw that a huge chunk of coral had plugged the hole in the *Endeavour*'s hull. Had the hole stayed open, neither fothering nor pumping could have saved their lives.

It took six weeks to repair the ship and make it seaworthy. There was plenty of fresh water from a river Cook named the Endeavour, and a fine supply of fish, birds, and greens for the crew's mess. The men collected mussels, each one so huge it could easily feed two men, and 300-pound turtles that made excellent eating.

Gathering plants and describing animals became a favorite pastime. One seaman reported a creature that looked like "the Devil and had 2 horns on its head."[10] It was almost certainly a giant fruit bat, also called a "flying fox." Another found a clamshell "so large he got into it & it fairly held him."[11] Banks examined eight-foot-high anthills, collected black and white ants, caught colorful butterflies, and gathered unusual seashells. He discovered a fish that actually travels on dry land by leaping like a frog, using its fins for feet—the mudskipper, a strange fish that can breathe air.

Most intriguing of all was the long-tailed animal whose giant leaps made it faster than Banks's greyhounds. Lieutenant Gore shot this unique Australian animal, the kangaroo, and it provided a tasty dinner. Banks kept the skull and skin for his scientific collection.

Cook spent four months charting two thousand miles of Australia's east coast. He claimed the entire eastern part for Britain, naming it New South Wales. (He conceded that the

The first picture of a kangaroo was published in 1773 in *Voyages*, Hawkesworth's fanciful account of Cook's first voyage.

west coast belonged to Holland because it had been discovered by the Dutch.) Cook theorized that Australia might be larger than all of Europe, but he did not describe it as a continent.

On August 6, 1770, the *Endeavour* began its long journey home. First it headed for Batavia, a port on the East Indian island of Java (now Jakarta, Indonesia). It had been a Dutch trading post since 1617 and was a popular destination for refitting ships and purchasing provisions.

One week before reaching Batavia the *Endeavour*'s officers visited Dutch ships that were anchored off the coast of Java. They heard disturbing news: "that the government in England were in utmost disorder, the people crying up & down the Streets Down with King George . . . that the Americans had refus'd to pay taxes of any kind in consequence of which was a large force being sent there both of sea and land forces."[12] Expanding the British Empire into the Pacific seemed more important than ever to make up for the possible loss of American colonies.

A Healthy Crew

Cook was proud of an unusual record. None of his men had died of illness during the entire voyage. He was a fanatic about good nutrition. At the beginning of the voyage he had punished two men to demonstrate his strictness about diet as important to general health. They'd received "12 lashes each for refusing to take their allowance of fresh Beef."[13] Cook realized that a healthy diet prevented scurvy, a sickness that had turned oceangoing vessels into "hospital ships" and "death ships." During long voyages many died, and survivors agonized in pain as their teeth loosened or fell out, their joints swelled, and their bodies became covered with sores. Citrus fruits as a cure for scurvy had been recommended as early as 1753 by Dr. James Lind, a British naval surgeon.

However, his recommendations were largely disregarded by the Admiralty and its officers.

Convinced that a proper diet prevented scurvy, Cook not only had a large stock of orange and lemon syrups, but he also experimented with sauerkraut, a pickled cabbage. Some 7,860 pounds of it were in the ship's hold, enough for two pounds per week per person for one year. When first served, the crew refused it as a horrible dish. However, after Cook ordered the sauerkraut "dressed every Day for the Cabbin Table" and told his officers to follow his example and eat it eagerly, sailors soon decided it was delicious, "the finest stuff in the World."[14] By adopting new foods rich in vitamin C he had prevented scurvy, the sailor's scourge.

Cook's obsession with cleanliness undoubtedly prevented other ailments. Bedding was aired daily. He even "examin'd the peoples hands—those who had dirty were punish'd by stopping their daily allowance of Grog."[15]

Port of Death

The *Endeavour* reached Batavia on October 11, 1770, six weeks after leaving the Australian coast. Open sewers and stinking, garbage-filled canals made this city a cesspool that bred killing diseases, such as malaria and dysentery. Within twelve days Cook, Banks, and most of the crew became seriously sick. Within ten weeks Tupia, his servant Tayeto, Dr. Monkhouse, and four others were dead, while forty crew members were bedded down, too weak to work.

As soon as the *Endeavour* had been repaired by Dutchmen and their slaves, Cook set sail. Even though almost everyone was ill, Cook was glad to leave "the unwholsome air of Batavia." The port was a death trap. Dutch captains at Batavia told him they were amazed that more than half his men were still alive.[16]

The death toll was horrifying. It became routine to conduct services on deck and bury someone at sea. During the ten-week trip to the Cape of Good Hope, twenty-two died, including Green, the astronomer, and Parkinson, the artist; four more died after the *Endeavour* had reached Cape Town. Cook had to hire men in Cape Town in order to sail the *Endeavour* back to England.

By July 12, 1771, two years and eleven months after leaving England, the *Endeavour* was home again. Cook had brilliantly fulfilled his instructions. Although he had not found the Unknown Southern Continent—and he doubted its existence—he had mapped vast areas of the Pacific and brought back charts of New Zealand and Australia that proved to be astonishingly accurate.[17] His expedition was the first to observe and comment in detail about Pacific cultures and the first to emphasize the importance of studying natural history in faraway lands.

Banks's artist, Sydney Parkinson, who died after leaving Batavia

6 · "MR. BANK'S TRIP"

BANKS WAS the hero of the hour. Newspapers called the expedition "Mr. Banks's trip." Cook was just the navigator who had steered a celebrity around the world. The *Westminster Journal* reported that Banks had brought back "no less than seventeen thousand plants of a kind never before seen." (He had actually returned with about one thousand.) The *Public Advertiser* informed its readers that as a result of discoveries made by Mr. Banks, "'tis expected that the Territories of Great Britain will be widely extended." The *London Evening Post* heralded the *Endeavour* expedition as sensational because it had "discovered a Southern Continent" whose people were "hospitable, ingenious, and civil."[1]

The nobility kept calling at Banks's elegant home to hear about his adventures, examine his tattoo, scrutinize a preserved human head, and marvel at the countless "curiosities" that included insects, animal skeletons, weapons, and costumes. They enjoyed hearing him rave about the beautiful Tahitian women and rant against the man-eating "savages" of New Zealand. It was delectable to listen to descriptions of dinners where dog, kangaroo, crow, or albatross had been eaten.

King George invited Banks to the royal palace. The glamorous adventurer presented His Majesty with a crown of gold and feathers once worn by a South American chief. To honor his great accomplishments, Oxford University gave Banks an honorary degree, and the great artist Sir Joshua Reynolds painted his portrait. Benjamin Franklin, in London

Joseph Banks painted by Benjamin West

as an agent for several American colonies, was fascinated when he attended a dinner party honoring Banks. He was heartily amused to learn about natives who didn't consider the "civilized" English superior and weren't interested in receiving their gifts.

The "celebrated Mr. Banks" was called the genius of the Pacific expedition, "the glory of England and the whole world."[2] He was even considered an authority in geography. His continued belief in the existence of the Unknown Southern Continent led to newspaper reports that the government would supply him with ships "to pursue his discoveries in the South Seas" and possibly establish a colony there.[3]

There was no fanfare for Cook. He returned to his wife, Elizabeth, and their two young sons, James and Nathaniel, at their modest home in the unfashionable village of Mile End. It must have been a sad homecoming, for during his absence two of his children had died: Elizabeth, who would have been four, and Joseph, a baby born after his departure.[4]

Cook delivered his charts, maps, and journals to the Admiralty. He also gave a collection of "curiosities": carved images, weapons, musical instruments, headdresses, and capes. Naval officials were impressed, because many new lands had been discovered and claimed for the Crown.

Cook had also demonstrated that sea voyages lasting years were feasible. Scurvy need no longer be the dreaded disease that frequently killed half a crew within a year. This self-schooled farmer's son had found an answer to survival during long explorations. His accomplishment could be compared to diet and health measures that make twentieth-century astronauts' journeys in spaceships possible.

As a reward for his remarkable accomplishments, the Admiralty made him a commander. Cook visited the king, who wanted a firsthand explanation of his charts and a private report of the voyage. Although not famous in the public eye, his brilliance was acknowledged not only by officials in the

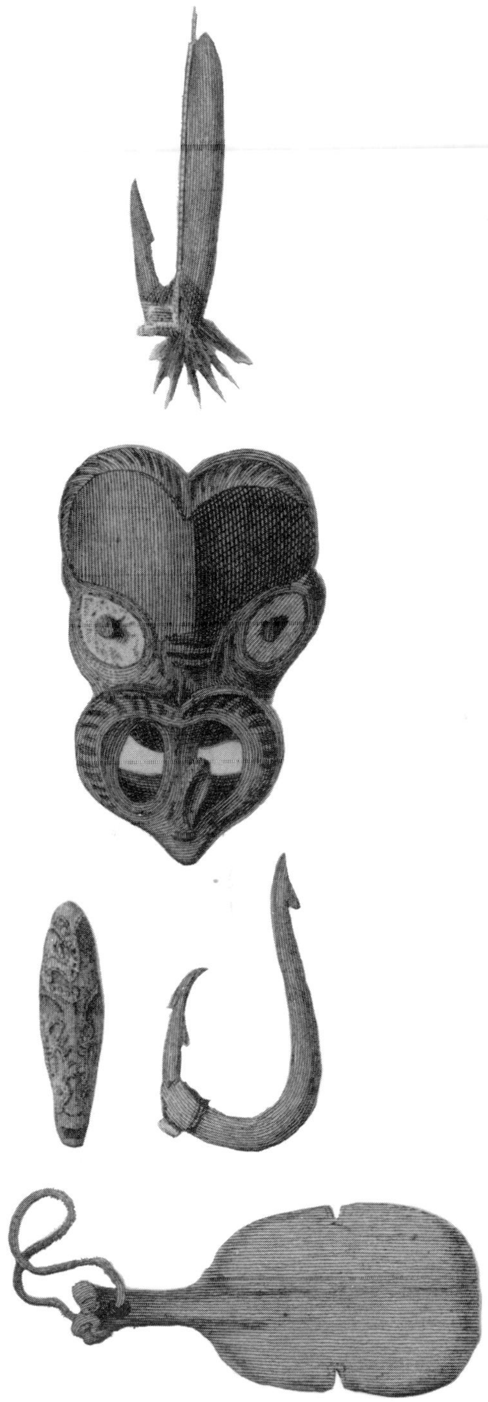

Artifacts collected in the South Pacific

Captain Cook

navy but also by members of the Royal Society, where he was invited to speak about his journey.

However, England's eminent scientist Alexander Dalrymple blamed Cook for failing to find the Unknown Southern Continent. How dare this lower-class, poorly schooled sailor conclude that it didn't exist? It *was* out there somewhere. Cook was so incompetent he didn't find it! Dalrymple demanded that another Pacific voyage be made, and he wished that the Admiralty would choose a more qualified captain.

Cook hoped he would be able to conduct another voyage. Although skeptical, his mind was still open to the possibility of finding the Southern Continent not yet Discovered. There were still vast areas in the Pacific he wanted to investigate. Banks, a pro-continent advocate, was also eager to sail again.

The Admiralty approved Cook's plans to circumnavigate the world by sailing the South Atlantic, the Indian Ocean, and the South Pacific. Using New Zealand and Tahiti as bases, he would spend two southern summers in latitudes never before investigated. It was to be the world's first Antarctic expedition.

Cook was to have two ships, the *Resolution* and the *Adventure*. Two ships made sense, for they could assist each other in case one was trapped on a reef or attacked by natives. Banks, accompanied by his own naturalists and artists, was to be part of the expedition. The voyage would have scientific significance, and Cook, who had always worked happily and harmoniously with Banks, undoubtedly looked forward to his stimulating company.

Banks arranged to take the following people with him: a naturalist, an astronomer, a painter, two horn players, three draftsmen, two secretaries, and six servants. Cook had to give up his captain's cabin to accommodate them, and a separate roundhouse was built on the *Resolution*'s deck for Banks's use.

As a result of the alterations, when the *Resolution* left dry dock to sail down the Thames River, she was so top-heavy that the pilot feared the ship would capsize. Cook pronounced her unsafe, and the Admiralty removed Banks's roundhouse. Banks was so upset "he swore and stamp'd . . . like a Mad Man; and instantly ordered his servants and all his things out of the Ship."[5] But rather than remain in London, Banks chartered a private ship and took his group to Iceland.

Despite this disappointment, Banks remained Cook's friend and admirer. As for Cook, he was indebted to Banks, who taught him the importance of having artists and scientists on board. Together they had established a tradition that was to be carried on by future explorers. During his second voyage Cook would not only look for a continent and investigate the Antarctic but also employ artists who could depict people, sights, and specimens with accuracy, and he would use scientists to study everything from stars to sea.

1772-1775

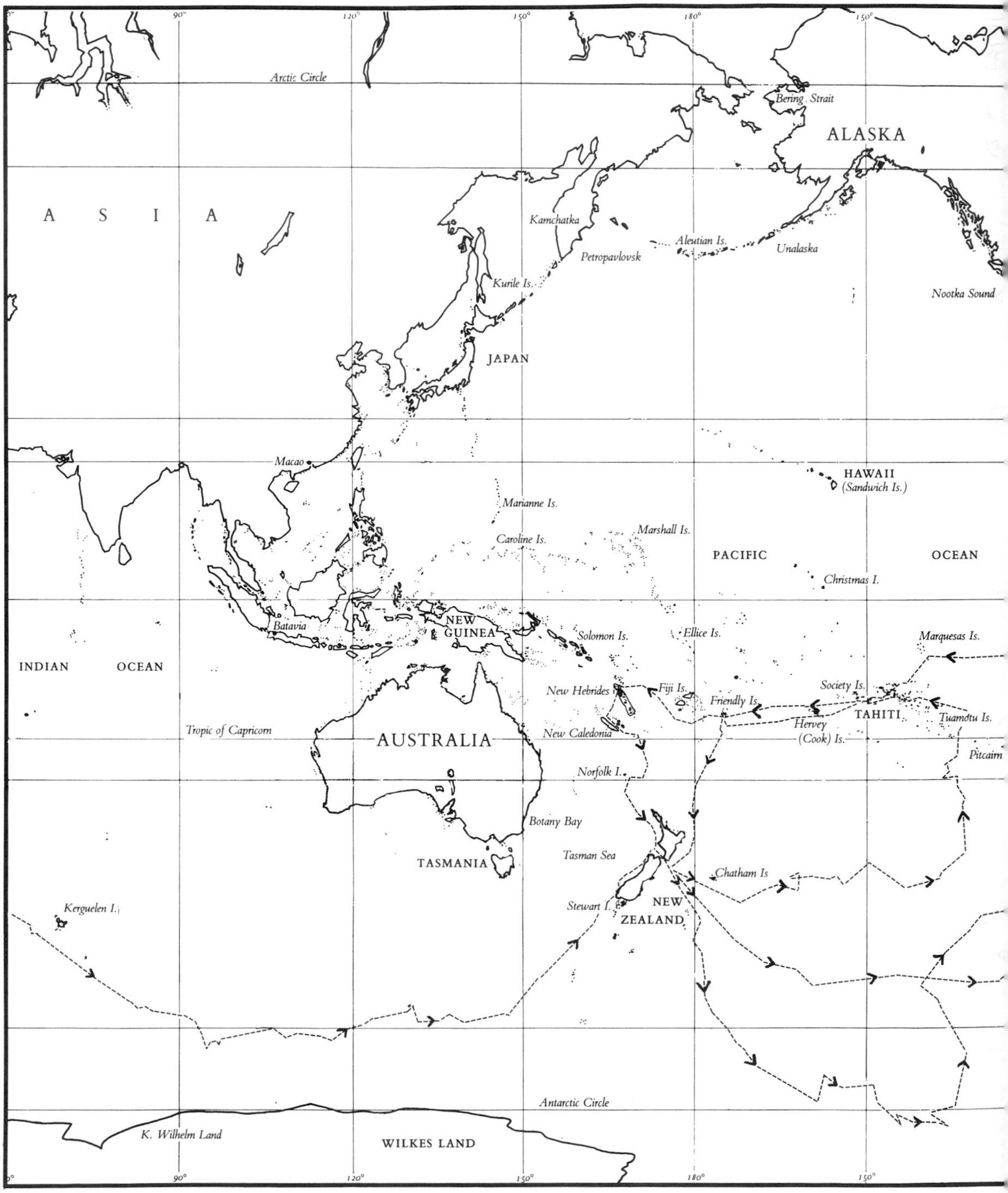
90°
120°
150°
180°
150°
Arctic Circle
Bering Strait
ALASKA
A S I A
Kamchatka
Aleutian Is.
Petropavlovsk
Unalaska
Kurile Is.
Nootka Sound
JAPAN
Macao
HAWAII
(Sandwich Is.)
Marianne Is.
Caroline Is.
Marshall Is.
PACIFIC
OCEAN
Christmas I.
Batavia
NEW
GUINEA
Solomon Is.
Ellice Is.
Marquesas Is.
INDIAN
OCEAN
New Hebrides
Fiji Is.
Society Is.
Friendly Is.
TAHITI
Tropic of Capricorn
Hervey
(Cook) Is.
Tuamotu Is.
AUSTRALIA
New Caledonia
Pitcairn
Norfolk I.
Botany Bay
TASMANIA
Tasman Sea
Chatham Is
Kerguelen I.
Stewart I.
NEW
ZEALAND
Antarctic Circle
K. Wilhelm Land
WILKES LAND
90°
120°
150°
180°
150°

The Second Voyage

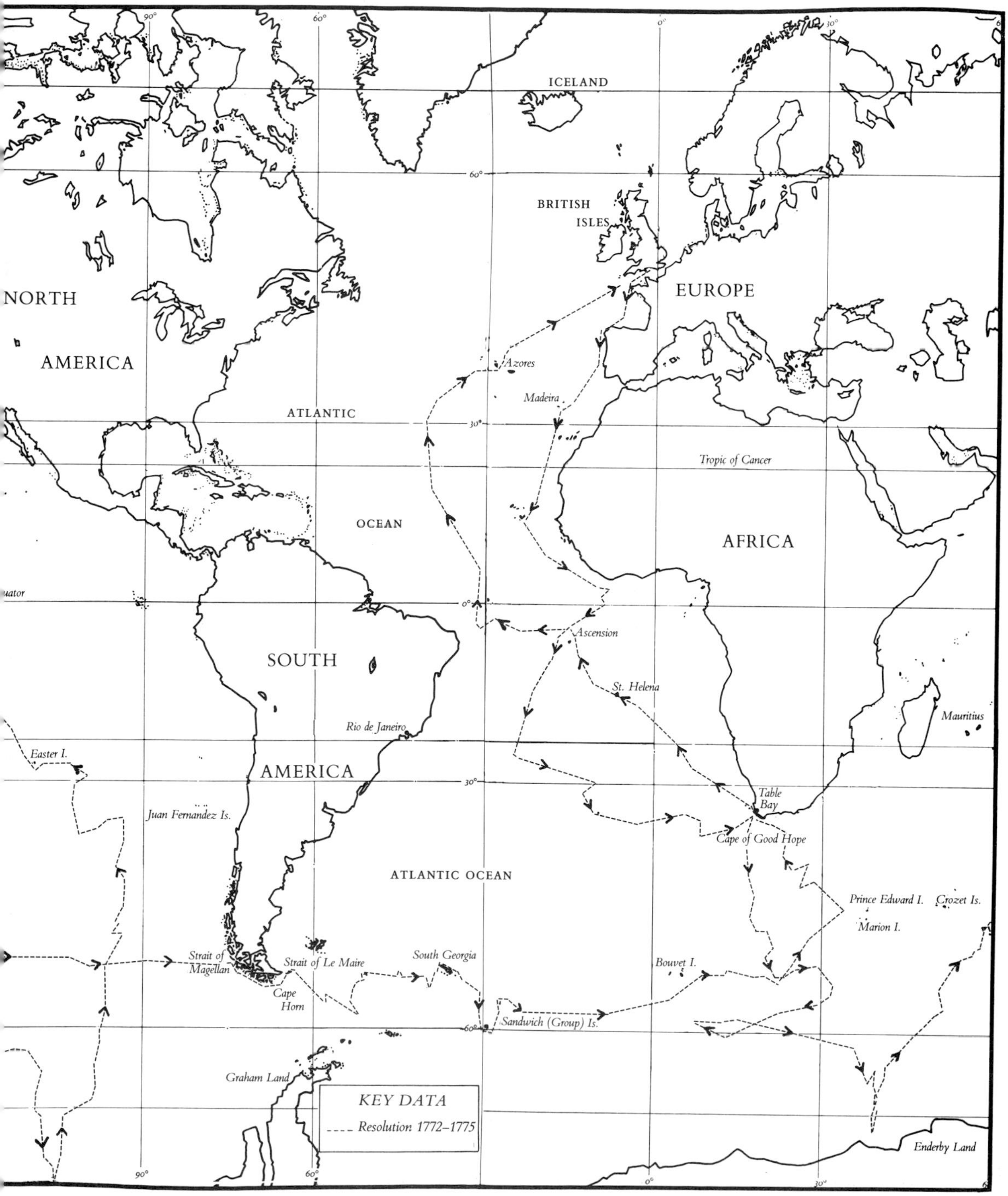

John Forster and his son George were naturalists on the second voyage.

7 · SECOND QUEST FOR CONTINENT

TWENTY VETERANS from the *Endeavour* were keen to serve under Cook again. However, recruiting the rest of the crew wasn't easy. The ordinary sailor didn't want to sail to the other end of the world, risking his life for little pay. To lure enough hands, sailors were advanced two months' salary.

Cook took charge of the *Resolution*. Tobias Furneaux, who had sailed around the world as a lieutenant under Wallis, was commander of the *Adventure*. Astronomers William Bayly and William Wales were on board, each able and amiable. Landscape painter William Hodges was chosen by Cook to replace an artist who had left with Banks. Unfortunately, the choice of John Forster to replace Banks as chief naturalist was a mistake. He proved to be a disagreeable, quarrelsome man, a chronic complainer who griped that his cabin was too small, criticized Cook's "overbearing" manner, disdained most of the officers, and viewed the crew as vulgar, immoral know-nothings. Although he received £4,000, a huge amount of money at that time and much more than Cook earned, Forster was piqued because he felt underpaid. (Cook's pay of six shillings a day came to less than £500 for the entire three-year voyage.) At least Forster's assistant, his seventeen-year-old son, George, was a likable fellow.

Captain Tobias Furneaux

Mariners knew how to figure latitude, the distance north and south of the equator, a location easily recognized because day and night are of equal length there. But finding longitude, the position east and west on the globe, was the navigator's nagging problem. Computing it by observing the stars was often so inaccurate that navigators were sometimes off the mark by hundreds of miles. On his first trip Cook used dead reckoning to measure longitude. That is, he estimated the ocean's current, the ship's speed, and the latitude.

A clock that could withstand the ship's rolling and extreme changes of temperature was needed to find longitude quickly and easily. By comparing England's time with local ship time, longitude could be accurately determined. Local time could be obtained by observing the sun and stars. On his second voyage Cook took along four precision clocks called chronometers. These "watch machines" were set to keep Greenwich, England, time. The astronomers wound these watches every day. Of the four, only one timepiece, devised by a self-educated carpenter named John Harrison, proved successful. The model had taken seventeen years to construct. It proved to be so accurate that it lost less than eight minutes after three years at sea. This "trusty guide" made Cook the first ship's commander in history to know his exact location with speed and precision.

This chronometer is an exact copy of the Kendall timepiece used by Cook.

Cook sailed from Plymouth on July 13, 1772, precisely one year and one day after returning from the first expedition. His orders were to sail toward the Antarctic in search of Cape Circumcision, a place named in honor of a religious feast day. It had been discovered in 1739 by the French explorer Louis Bouvet, who was sure he had found the Unknown Southern Continent. However, dense fog and a frozen sea kept Bouvet from landing. Cook consulted a chart published by Dalrymple showing Bouvet's route.

Icebergs and Ice Fields

The *Resolution* and *Adventure* headed directly south into unknown frozen waters, into a seascape no one could have imagined. The waters were crammed with masses of ice, called floes, small icebergs called growlers (they groaned and crackled), enormous ice fields, and mountainous icebergs, some two miles wide and two hundred feet high. Chunks sliding off the bergs sounded like cannon shots and thunder. As the ships pushed south, more than one hundred icebergs were counted in one day.

The *Resolution* and *Adventure*, surrounded by icebergs

Sails froze so that they were hard as metal. Ropes felt like sharp wires. Handling iron-hard ropes caused bloody, frost-bitten hands. Some days the excessive cold was agonizing, and "arms in a very short space of time put on the appearance of icicles, and became so numbed as . . . to be totally incapable of use."[1]

Spectacular panoramas of ice islands were awesome. The only signs of life were whales, seabirds, and plenty of penguins, some seen marching like soldiers three abreast in regular formation. The sight of these creatures was not only a source of amusement but of hope, because the crew assumed that penguins never wandered far from land. They did not know that penguins can live far out at sea for months at a time.

To get drinking water, men set out in boats and hacked off blocks of ice. When hauled onto the ships, then melted in copper caldrons, the water was sweet, without a trace of salt from the briny sea. Fresh water seemed to be a sign that land was nearby. No one realized that the water was fresh because icebergs are chunks of glaciers that originated on land but can float hundreds of miles out to sea. (Glaciers are masses of moving ice formed from compacted snow.)

Cook was the first man to sail across the Antarctic Circle. During January of 1773, he came within seventy-five miles of the Antarctic continent. After his determined search, he concluded that Cape Circumcision wasn't land at all; it was the top of an iceberg.[2] Although he theorized that a great continent could exist beyond the walls of solid ice, he could no longer risk having his ships locked forever in a frozen sea. Even though this was southern summer, temperatures were below zero, snow or sleet was constant, furious gales frequent, and fogs were blinding.

In February the *Adventure* disappeared in fog. Fortunately, due to Cook's foresight, Furneaux had charts and instructions that designated Queen Charlotte's Sound, New Zealand, as

Chopping ice to be melted for drinking water

a meeting place should they be separated. It was a thousand miles away.

Ports in the South Seas

On March 26, 1773, the *Resolution* anchored at Dusky Bay, New Zealand, where the men rested for six weeks before joining the *Adventure* at Queen Charlotte's Sound.

Cook was shocked to find that many of Furneaux's men had scurvy. Furneaux, obviously, had not been strict about diet. Cook was so upset that he immediately sent his men out and went himself to gather "sellery and Scurvey grass and other vegetables." He gave orders that this should be boiled "with Wheat or Oatmeal and Portable Soups for the Crew of both Sloops every morning for breakfast and also with Pease every day for dinner."[3] Within weeks, the scurvy patients were cured.

Cook planted gardens and let pigs, sheep, and goats loose. He not only wanted to make the place a worthwhile stopover for provisioning ships, but he also hoped the inhabitants would take up gardening and farming. By doing so he expected they would work the soil like English country folk—a goal really not suitable for them.

In June the two ships set out once again, looking for a sign of the Southern Continent not yet Discovered. After weeks at sea, some men on the *Adventure* again contracted scurvy. Furneaux still didn't understand the importance of diet. And despite his strictness, even Cook's ship had a few mild cases. Therefore Cook stopped his quest for a continent and sailed to Tahiti.

Swarms of girls swam through the surf, climbed on board,

When this Maori chieftain visited the *Resolution*, Hodges painted his picture.

and greeted sailors with open arms. Native men honored the captain by wrapping him in reams of colored cloths. He stood sweltering for hours, stiff as a mummy, while the Tahitians performed seemingly endless welcoming ceremonies. Natives played nose flutes and sailors played bagpipes to celebrate their reunion. Everyone was elated except Forster. He was disgusted by the girls' "loose morals," and he usually disapproved whenever Cook participated in "savage customs."

Playing the nose flute

The sick were housed in tents set up in Fort Venus. Since the *Endeavour*'s visit four years earlier, two wars had taken place, and many of Cook's old friends had been killed. "Queen" Purea had lost her power and was miserably poor. A young man named Tu was now head chief. Breadfruit wasn't in season, and few provisions were offered for sale. Therefore, after a stay of only seventeen days, the ships sailed on to nearby islands, where two native men joined them. One was Odiddy, who would act as Cook's interpreter. He was so well liked by the *Resolution*'s crew that they were sorry to see him leave the following June, when he returned to his island. The other was an intriguing fellow called Mai. Furneaux insisted upon taking him to England, where he was bound to create a sensation.

In September Cook headed west, looking for land. He rediscovered Amsterdam and Middleburg, islands that Dutch navigator Abel Tasman had briefly visited 130 years earlier, in 1643. Cook renamed them the Friendly Islands because of the hearty welcome he received. (They are now called the Tongan Islands.) He toasted friendship by drinking kava. Natives made it by chewing roots of kava plants, then spitting the juice into a bowl. Although kava was passed around, Cook boasted that he was the only one of his group who drank it.

After stocking up on fruits, fowl, and other foods, Cook rubbed noses with the chiefs and presented them with bags

Boats of the Friendly Islanders

of English garden seeds. He was refreshed and ready to renew his explorations in the deep freeze of the Antarctic.

To break up the long journey, Cook chose New Zealand as a stopover. A furious gale separated the ships. Once again the *Adventure* was lost.

When Cook docked at Queen Charlotte's Sound, he waited three weeks for the *Adventure*. During that time his men found human thigh bones and a head—the remains of a cannibal feast. Once again Cook watched islanders eating broiled human flesh "with seeming good relish before the whole ships Company."[4] Although revolted, Cook did not condemn cannibalism, excusing it as a custom of people who had not been exposed to European civilization.

Before leaving, Cook left instructions for Furneaux buried in a bottle under a tree with the words "Look Underneath" carved on its bark.

The *Adventure* did finally arrive a few days after Cook had left. Furneaux found the bottled instructions that described

Cook's planned course. But bedraggled and battered from rough storms, Furneaux realized his men needed to rest for a few days. He sent ten men to gather wild greens. They never returned. Furneaux sent a party to find them. What they found was horrifying: the head of a ship's servant, the tattooed hands of two seamen, five shoes that belonged to the group, and baskets filled with human flesh made ready for the cooking pit.

Revenge was risky. Furneaux quickly lifted anchor and headed for England by way of Cape Horn and the Cape of Good Hope. He reached home on July 14, 1774, one year before the *Resolution*—just in time to become commander of a warship to be used against the American revolutionaries.

Return to the Antarctic

After leaving New Zealand, Cook set his course for the southeast, resuming his search for new lands. He crossed the Antarctic Circle twice more, each time retreating because he was barricaded by ice.

Counting icebergs and watching penguins' antics wasn't amusing anymore, because many of the men became ill. Captain Cook was seriously sick with a stomach ailment, "to the grief of all the ship's company," who feared he might die.[5] In this instance John Forster showed compassion. He offered a unique medicine: His pet dog, acquired in Tahiti, was boiled so that the ailing captain could regain his strength by eating dog stew. The captain ate it, but his recovery was slow. It took weeks before he was as strong, stubborn, and strict as ever.

Although Cook felt he had traveled south "farther than any man had been before . . . as far as . . . [he thought] possible for man to go" he was intent upon sweeping through the southern Atlantic the following year for a final search.[6]

A native snatched Hodges's hat from his head while he was making a sketch for this painting, *Moments of Easter Island.*

Island Hopping

On March 11, 1774, after 103 days at sea, the *Resolution* reached Easter Island, that fascinating land where hundreds of stone heads still dominate the landscape. Easter Island had been discovered in 1722 by the Dutch admiral Jacob Roggeveen, who reportedly saw twelve-foot men and the relatively petite eleven-foot women. The stone heads range in height from fifteen to thirty-five feet, some weighing up to fifty tons.

Island natives were at a loss to explain the existence of these mammoth sculptures. Archaeologists are still puzzled by Easter Island statues—when they were built, what they signified, and how people could have made such huge, heavy statues without modern tools remain a mystery. Cook "could not help wondering how they were set up, indeed if the Island was once Inhabited by a race of Giants 12 feet high."[7]

After a few days, Cook set his course for the Marquesas, islands which had not been seen by Europeans since the Spanish navigator Mendana had massacred two hundred of their natives in 1595. Despite inaccurate charts, Cook found the Marquesas. He thought the islanders "as fine a race of people as any in this Sea; for a fine shape and regular features, they perhaps surpass all other Nations." Lieutenant Charles Clerke agreed, saying that the inhabitants were "the most beautiful race of People [he] ever beheld."[8] The islanders gladly exchanged fish, fruit, and pigs for some red parrot feathers that had been stocked on board. The crew had learned that these were more valuable than gold in the South Seas.

As soon as Cook had charted the precise position of the Marquesas, he sailed on to Tahiti. This island that Europeans had idealized as near perfect was preparing to attack its neighbors. An impressive armada of huge war canoes was being assembled to sail against the nearby island of Moorea. Ac-

A Tahitian war fleet

cording to Cook's estimates there were close to eight thousand fighters. He counted 160 elaborately carved canoes, ranging in size from fifty to ninety feet long, and an equal number of small canoes carrying provisions. Thousands of warriors were armed with stones, clubs, and pikes.

Cook refused the request that his ship join the Tahitians in battle. He was fascinated by their preparations but disappointed because a sea fight didn't take place during his seven-week stay.

Once again, there were Tahitians who wanted to journey to England—possibly *their* vision of paradise. But Cook refused all passengers. He convinced Odiddy to leave the expedition by warning him he might never have another chance to return to his homeland. Mai was to be the only traveler, and he was on Furneaux's ship.

Tahiti proved so alluring for gunner's mate John Marra that he tried to desert. Marra, who was caught swimming toward shore, was placed in irons, then released when the *Resolution* was at sea. After learning that Marra had neither family nor friends in any part of the world, Cook was sympathetic. "Where can such a Man spend his days better than at one of these isles," Cook wrote, "where he can injoy all the necessaries and some of the luxuries of life in ease and Plenty."[9]

After revisiting the Friendly Islands, the *Resolution* proceeded south. It left the vast area occupied by Polynesians and entered a new world, the world of Melanesia, occupied by short, dark-skinned natives with thick lips, flat noses, and curly hair.[10] By European standards they were ugly, and they spoke languages no one could understand. Many Melanesians, on the other hand, were repelled by the pale-skinned Englishmen, suspecting they must be spirits of the dead because they weren't the dark color of human beings.

The expedition explored New Hebrides. Good relations were marred only once, when a sentry shot and killed a native man for no apparent reason. New Caledonia, the fourth-largest island in the Pacific, was an important new discovery. Its people shunned gifts of clothing, preferring the comfort of their own nudity. Unarmed, they were unafraid, even though—or because—they had never seen Europeans before. These natives were so gentle and friendly that Cook wished he could stay longer than sixteen days, but it was September, and he had to make another stab toward the South Pole during the southern summer months. Before leaving, Cook gave away pigs and dogs for breeding and claimed the land for England.

A New Caledonian. The piece of cord on his hat was used for throwing lances.

In October of 1774, Cook stopped at Queen Charlotte's Sound, in New Zealand, to stock wood and water before penetrating the icy seas. After refitting the *Resolution*, the men were prepared for their final trip to the Antarctic. This time Cook headed toward Cape Horn to examine the South Atlantic. He had to confirm or disprove Dalrymple's chartings of the Unknown Southern Continent.

The *Resolution* covered 4,500 miles in five weeks before sighting South America on December 17, 1774. Cook explored and charted the frigid, desolate coastlines of Tierra del Fuego and Cape Horn. During the first week in January 1775, Cook entered the Atlantic.

Once again an area that Dalrymple's charts had designated as land was ocean. However, shortly after leaving the Horn, land was found and named South Georgia. It proved to be an island "where it did not seem probable that any one would ever be benifited by the descovery."[11] Ice prevented Cook from landing on other islands, which he named the South Sandwich Islands.

There seemed to be no merit in discovering a country "doomed by Nature never once to feel the warmth of the Suns rays, but to lie for ever buried under everlasting snow and ice."[12] "The Southern Hemisphere [has been] sufficiently explored and a final end put to the searching after a Southern

Continent," wrote Cook. Nevertheless, he conceded "that there may be a Continent or large tract of land near the Pole. . . . I am of the opinion there is, and it is probable that we have seen part of it."[13]

Proud of his loyal crew who he felt would cheerfully go wherever he led them, Cook felt that prolonging his voyage might affect his men's health.[14] After a five-week rest at the Cape of Good Hope, the *Resolution* reached England.

His second voyage proved to the world that James Cook was one of history's greatest navigators. The Pacific Ocean was the last great space on earth for the most part unexplored by Europeans. No one could conceive that one-third of our globe is covered by its waters. It is twice as large as the Atlantic Ocean, and bigger than all the land surface on earth. By accurately charting enormous areas of the Pacific Ocean, Cook had discovered water space that enlarged estimates about the earth's size.

Cook was impressed by the variety of boats made by the Friendly Islanders.

Through the use of a chronometer that accurately determined longitude, he rediscovered "lost" islands. He also discovered new lands and learned about societies that Europeans had never before encountered. As for that age-old notion about a fertile, rich continent that anchored the earth, he exposed it as myth.

The voyage had taken three years and eighteen days. During that time the expedition had sailed more than 70,000 miles. Cook noted proudly that despite the long voyage, only four of his men had died: three because of accidents (two were drowned, and one was killed in a fall) and one from sickness not related to scurvy. No one had died from scurvy—a spectacular record!

8 · INTERLUDE IN ENGLAND

THE SECOND VOYAGE didn't seem terribly important to the public. Cook had failed to find a continent, and even though he had drastically changed the image of the Antarctic and Pacific oceans, his accomplishments didn't make headlines.

Journalists concentrated on more momentous news: American colonists were revolting against British rule, and troops were being shipped across the Atlantic to fight them.

As for the South Seas, newspapers had been featuring an abundance of information, based upon a runaway bestseller about the first expedition called *Voyages*, by John Hawkesworth. Although the journals of both Cook and Banks were at his disposal, Hawkesworth had concocted false and fanciful stories. He had ignored geographical accomplishments but provided luscious descriptions of free love and beautiful women—a good way to guarantee his book's success.

When Furneaux's *Adventure* arrived in England exactly one year before Cook's return, its crew added more exciting stories about grand panoramas, gorgeous people, and gory customs. There were native weapons and costumes—and, most sensational of all, a real, live South Seas island native: Mai, the presumed prince of a tropical island paradise!

Mai, "Noble Savage"

Joseph Banks volunteered to adopt Mai, become his interpreter, and act as his chaperone. Viewed as a rare specimen of humanity, Mai was brought to the palace and presented to the king. He visited the House of Lords, was exhibited at the Royal Society, and sailed on a yacht belonging to the Admiralty. The nobility competed among themselves to have this Polynesian prince as their house guest. Dressed in elegant English fashions, he became an affected fop who exuded charm, knowing when to bow and how to kiss ladies' hands. Mai attended the opera and theater and was seen at society's most sumptuous banquets. He enjoyed hunting parties and was proud that he bagged so many birds, though most of these proved to be privately owned barnyard chickens. He couldn't learn to ride horseback and claimed he was much too busy to learn English. Nevertheless, London socialites found him enchanting.

Writers glorified Mai as a "noble savage" who was virtuous and happy because he had not been exposed to the vices and corrupting influences of civilization.[1] The famous

British actors in elaborate, fanciful costumes played Mai and Purea.

Mai, painted by Joshua Reynolds

artist Sir Joshua Reynolds painted him elegantly dressed in turban and robes—a fashion neither English nor Tahitian. Poems were composed about him, and a ridiculous play that depicted Mai as the future king of Tahiti reflected the romantic image he projected.[2]

Not everyone was enchanted. There were some who declared that Mai should learn a trade and not waste his time acting the part of an idle socialite. Knowing that Mai was neither prince nor chief, Cook held a dim view of him, judging him to be a foolish, common fellow. Excitement about the visiting Tahitian eventually died down. Society became bored with Mai, and King George decided to send him home—one reason for a third voyage to the Pacific.

Although Cook was not popularly celebrated, the Admiralty was enormously impressed by his accomplishments. He was promoted to the rank of captain. The Royal Society not only elected him a Fellow but also presented him with the Copley gold medal as an award for his successful battle against scurvy.

To acknowledge his many years of service the Admiralty endowed him with a soft berth: a lifetime appointment as head of Greenwich Hospital, an institution for retired seamen. This easy, comfortable job would enable him to be home with his wife and sons. He would also have time to write his own account of his voyages—a project he was determined to do, since he had been upset by Hawkesworth's fictionalized best-seller about his first expedition.

However, after six months at home, Cook became bored by inactivity. He wrote to a friend, "a few Months ago the whole Southern hemisphere was hardly big enough for me and now I am going to be confined within the limits of Greenwich Hospital, which are far too small for an active mind like mine."[3] When told that the navy planned a third voyage to the Pacific, he enthusiastically volunteered to lead the expedition. The prime purpose of the expedition was to find a Northwest Passage.

A Northwest Passage

For three centuries after the discovery of America, European navigators had searched in vain for a waterway through or above Canada that would connect the Atlantic and Pacific oceans. Geographers were positive that an ice-free passage existed. Dalrymple envisioned one that connected Hudson Bay to the west coast. An inland sea covering much of today's British Columbia was a common feature on many eighteenth-century maps of the northern Pacific.

During the sixteenth century Juan de Fuca, a pilot for Spain, claimed to have sailed through a northwestern passage in only twenty days, past land that was rich in gold, silver, and pearls. Spanish mariners continued to sail northward. Although they never confirmed de Fuca's tale, they kept claiming more and more land along the California coastline.

Russia was another rival. By the eighteenth century its explorers, hunters, and fur trappers were in Alaska, aggressively investigating inland Arctic waterways. They were encroaching on North America too quickly for British comfort.

For England the Northwest Passage was of major importance. A peaceful, quick route to the fabulously profitable tea and silk trade of China could insure the prosperity of the British Empire. Its discovery was deemed so vital that in

Sketched during the Battle of Lexington and Concord

1745 the government established an award of £20,000 to the navigator who found it. Before Cook there had been at least fifty voyages in search of the Northwest Passage.[4]

By 1775, when the American Revolution began—the year of Lexington and Concord and Bunker Hill—England was especially troubled. The Northwest Passage to the Orient could make up for the possible loss of trade with the colonies. The Admiralty was confident that Cook could discover it.[5] Because eighteenth-century scientists were sure that an ocean could not freeze, Cook's ships were not equipped to protect them from ice. This is baffling, because Cook had reported the solid-ice conditions of the Antarctic.

In addition to finding the Northwest Passage, Cook was instructed "to carefully observe the nature of the Soil . . . the Animals and Fowls . . . the Fishes . . . and to make as accurate drawings of them as you can." He was to report "any Metals, Minerals, or valuable Stones . . . and observe the Genius, Temper, Disposition, and Number of Natives . . . and endeavour, by all proper means to cultivate a friendship with them."[6]

1776-1780

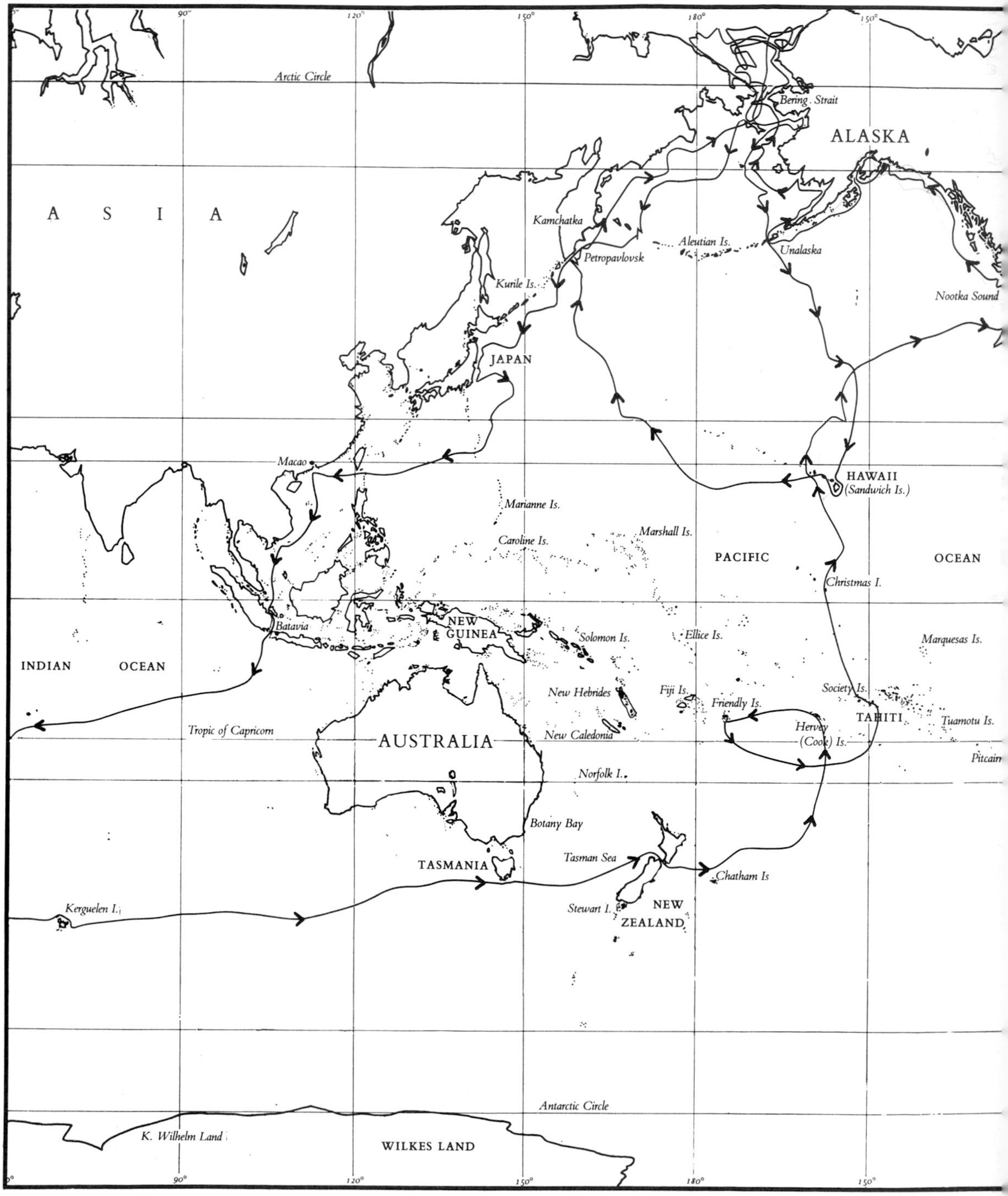

Arctic Circle
Bering Strait
ALASKA
A S I A
Kamchatka
Aleutian Is.
Petropavlovsk
Unalaska
Kurile Is.
Nootka Sound
JAPAN
Macao
HAWAII
(Sandwich Is.)
Marianne Is.
Marshall Is.
Caroline Is.
PACIFIC
OCEAN
Christmas I.
Batavia
NEW GUINEA
Solomon Is.
Ellice Is.
Marquesas Is.
INDIAN
OCEAN
New Hebrides
Fiji Is.
Friendly Is.
Society Is.
TAHITI
Tuamotu Is.
Tropic of Capricorn
AUSTRALIA
New Caledonia
Hervey (Cook) Is.
Pitcairn
Norfolk I.
Botany Bay
Tasman Sea
TASMANIA
Chatham Is
Kerguelen I.
Stewart I.
NEW ZEALAND
Antarctic Circle
K. Wilhelm Land
WILKES LAND
90°
120°
150°
180°

The Third Voyage

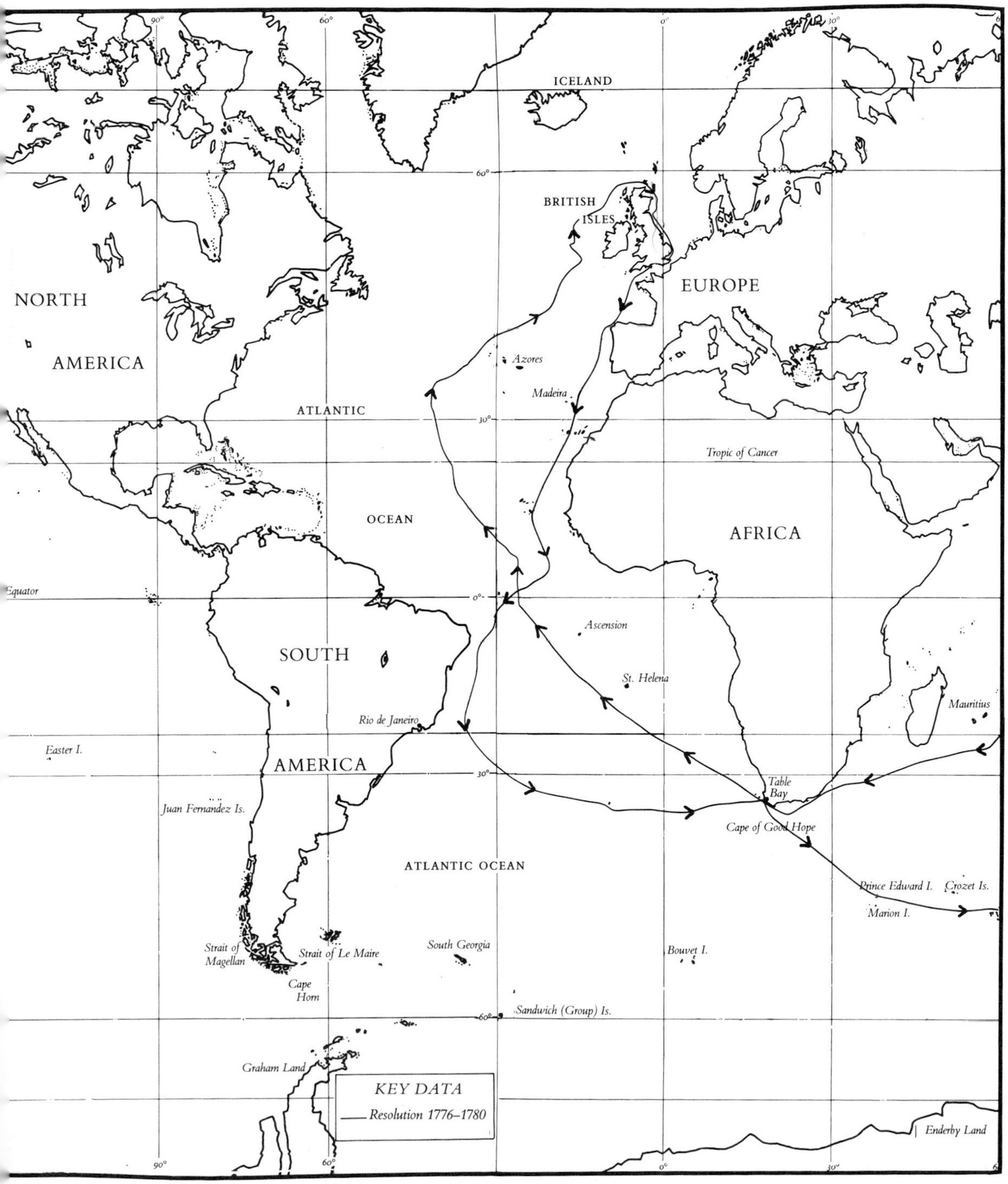

9·MAI BROUGHT HOME

Captain Charles Clerke

COOK'S THIRD VOYAGE was launched from Plymouth Harbor on July 12, 1776, eight days after the Declaration of Independence was adopted. His two ships, the *Resolution* and *Discovery*, both converted coal carriers, contrasted with the many mighty warships around him that held troops bound for America to fight the rebellious colonists.

Although refitted at the dockyards, the flagship *Resolution* leaked like a sieve, so that "hardly a Man . . . could lie dry in his bed; the officers in the gunroom were all driven out of their cabbins by Water that came thro' the sides."[1] The *Discovery*, commanded by Charles Clerke, was sturdy and strong. Clerke had been an outstanding officer on Cook's previous expeditions.

One hundred twelve men on the *Resolution* and seventy on the *Discovery* expected to be away from home for at least two years. Among them were seven American colonists: two from Connecticut and one each from Massachusetts, Pennsylvania, Virginia, South Carolina, and "America."[2] William Bayly, the astronomer, was once again part of the expedition, and a Swiss artist, John Webber, was appointed to illustrate strange lands and fascinating peoples.

Ships' holds were packed with supplies needed for a long voyage. Decks were jammed with animals that "Farmer King

George" wished to bestow upon his South Sea Island subjects. There were bulls, cows, sheep, goats, rabbits, turkeys, geese, ducks, peacocks, and hogs—many taken from His Majesty's private stock. The *Resolution* smelled and sounded like a barnyard. Cook quipped that his ship was a "Noah's Ark, lacking only a few females of our own species."[3]

Mai came aboard with an enormous cargo of his own. There was crockery and kitchenware, a substantial supply of port wine, an assortment of toys including tin soldiers and a jack-in-the-box, a globe of the world, a hand organ, a Bible, a collection of guns, a sword given to him by the king, and a complete suit of medieval armor. He expected to impress his countrymen with his possessions.

After the ships had reached Cape Town, South Africa, Mai gave up his cabin so that four horses could be crammed into it. He hoped that the animals were intended for his private Polynesian estate.

The next stopover was Kerguelen's Island, some two thousand miles southeast of the Cape of Good Hope. Named and discovered by the French, it was so bleak and barren that

William Ellis, the surgeon's second mate on the *Discovery*, painted Kerguelen's Island: Cook's crew called it the Island of Desolation.

Cook renamed it Island of Desolation. After spending a depressing Christmas there, the men occupied themselves clubbing seals and penguins—creatures that had not yet learned to fear men. The meat made poor eating, but the fat was used to make oil for the ships' lamps.

Cook was in urgent need of grass for the livestock. During most of January 1777, the ships sailed east. After enduring dense fogs and severe storms, the men were relieved to reach Van Diemen's Land (Tasmania) by the end of the month. But the place proved disappointing. There was not enough grass for the cattle, and the Tasmanians were unfriendly.[4] After several days they left for Queen Charlotte's Sound, New Zealand.

A Cannibal's Confession

This was the land where ten Englishmen of the second expedition had been killed and eaten. Suspecting that the *Resolution* and *Discovery* had arrived to revenge the slaughter, the Maoris hesitated to visit at first. But curiosity was stronger than fear, and they soon came on board. Sailors were amazed to watch them eat candles, including the wicks, and drink lamp oil (probably due to a lack of fat in their diet).

When the crew landed to set up tents and a scientific observatory, Maori families built makeshift houses to be nearby. The cannibals were sociable, but the sailors were wary. They were afraid of being eaten.

Everyone was surprised when Chief Kahoura visited Cook. This chief confessed that he was head of the party that had killed the ten men from Furneaux's boat. He even informed the captain that he alone had slaughtered most of them.

Acting as interpreter, Mai repeated Kahoura's description of the incident: Native people had taken a few biscuits while

Chief Kahoura asked to have his portrait painted.

Furneaux's shore party were eating. This made the sailors so angry that a fight ensued, during which master's mate John Rowe shot and killed two people. The fatal shootings enraged the Maoris. They clubbed, butchered, and ate Furneaux's men. Cook saw no reason for revenge, because the incident had been caused by a trigger-happy seaman.

Chief Kahoura felt so safe that, after eyeing a portrait that was hanging in Cook's cabin, he wanted one made of himself. His wish was granted. Instead of killing Chief Kahoura, who had led the massacre, Cook had him pose for the expedition's artist, John Webber, who painted his portrait!

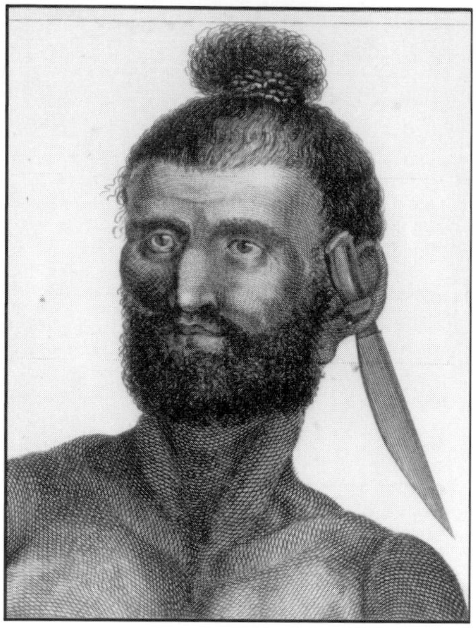

A man from the Cook Islands, named Mou'rooa, visited Cook's ships

Mai was allowed to hire a seventeen-year-old fatherless chieftain's son named Tiarooa to be his personal servant. Tiarooa, in turn, hired Koa, a youngster of ten to be *his* personal servant. At first Cook didn't want these boys to leave New Zealand because they would probably never be able to return home. But when he noted that "not one, even their nearest relations seemed to trouble themselves about what became of them," he allowed them to accompany Mai.[5]

On February 25, 1777, Cook sailed from New Zealand and headed for Tahiti, his designated resting place. On the way he discovered a group of islands some 600 miles west of Tahiti, now known as the Cook Islands. It was impossible to land on most of them because of wild surf and dangerous reefs.

However, since fodder for animals was a perpetual problem, sailors kept rowing to shore to gather grasses so that King George's livestock wouldn't starve.

Cruel Punishments

Because there wasn't enough animal feed to last until his ships reached Tahiti, Cook made a detour to the Friendly Islands (the Tongan Islands). Two months after leaving New Zealand the ships anchored there. The livestock grazed in lush pasture while camp was set up for a prolonged stay.

The British were treated as honored guests. Chief Fernau, who presented himself as ruler of 153 islands, welcomed Cook effusively. Chief Tapa had his "palace" carried on the shoulders of his subjects and set down near Cook's tents. Chief Fattafee came aboard the *Resolution*. At first he refused to visit Cook's cabin, because "if he went there people would walk over his head and this was never done."[6] Eventually curiosity won, and he went below deck.

All chiefs waived the usual signs of respect required from

their subjects. Cook's men were not expected to strip to the waist whenever a chief passed by. They did not have to bow their heads as low as a chief's feet. (Sometimes chiefs were considerate. They held up one of their legs so that people could bow without having to flop to the ground.)

The Friendly Islanders presented generous gifts, including a thirty-foot-high pile of breadfruit and yams topped by one baked and one live hog. More than one hundred men and women entertained the English by performing elaborate dances with amazing precision, while drums beat and huge choruses sang.

Cook, seated with his crew, watches dances on the Friendly Islands.

Boxing matches, at the Friendly Islands

Watching wrestling matches was so much fun that some sailors entered the ring and challenged the fighters. They were knocked down and laughed at by thousands in the audience. There were guffaws again when a shocked sailor who was trying to be gallant tried to stop a boxing bout between female contenders. The event continued, as "lusty wenches" fought "with [as] much art as the men."[7]

Staying at the Friendly Islands was a pure holiday. In beautiful surroundings, with delightful people who welcomed them, Cook's men freely strolled about the countryside. The islanders were so at ease that they constantly crowded onto the ships. Chiefs enjoyed razor-blade shaves from the crew's barbers. Officers anxious for a unique experience had their beards scraped off by natives using sharp shells and sharks' teeth.

Cook was fascinated by the ceremonies. He stripped to the waist, untied his hair so that it flowed over his shoulders, and sat cross-legged "in conformity to their custom" in order to attend their rituals.[8] Islanders were likewise intrigued by English customs. An astronomer's study of the heavens seemed like a religious observance, and the carefully guarded chronometers were judged to be holy magical objects.

There was only one infuriating problem. The islanders grabbed cats, tools, sailors' clothing, and whatever else intrigued them. Although the pilfered items were of no great value, Cook became so enraged that he not only took chiefs as hostages but also meted out brutal punishments. One culprit's arm was slashed with a knife; another had his ears cut off; and several (including a chief!) were flogged. Cook had always been a kind, humane man. His officers were shocked when he ordered these cruel punishments. They could not understand why their captain had become so ruthless.

After an eleven-week stay, Cook set out for Tahiti, where he intended to leave Mai, who expected to be greeted as a returning hero by his people. When the *Resolution* and *Discovery* reached Tahitian waters, however, islanders who boarded the ships didn't pay any attention to Mai. This native-turned-London-gentleman wasn't noticed until he took out his stash of red feathers. Tahitians crowded around Mai, anxious to barter almost anything in exchange for them. His popularity ended when his supply was used up.

Mai was ignored when he disembarked dressed in European finery. Tahitians were not impressed even when he stood on a special stage secured to a canoe cruising along the shore so that all could admire him wearing European medieval armor. Chiefs resented him, and commoners ignored him. Realizing that Mai was disliked, Captain Cook felt obligated to find another island home for him. However, there was no rush to leave Tahiti.

A Human Sacrifice

No one had imagined that human sacrifice was practiced in this earthly paradise, but Captain Cook, surgeon's mate Anderson, artist Webber, and Mai witnessed a gruesome ceremony. A battered man's body had been trussed to a pole and placed upon a platform. The victim was "a common fellow" whose head had been bashed in by a stone. While drums beat, priests recited prayers, used red feathers, pulled out tufts of the victim's hair, plucked out one of his eyes, and cooked a dog's entrails as part of their ritual. The elaborate ceremony was staged at this time because the Tahitians were preparing to attack a neighboring island, and they wanted to appease the war god Oro by offering a sacrifice.

Cook felt privileged "to see something of this extraordinary and Barbarous custom."[9] After the ceremony, however,

Cook and his officers witness a human sacrifice.

he told one of the chiefs that he was shocked because an innocent man had been murdered; that in England anyone who killed another person would be hanged. The chief was as horrified. Hanging someone! What a gruesome custom! How dare the English criticize a religiously inspired human sacrifice!

During a five-week stay, the sailors were treated to banquets, theatrical performances, and native dances. The crew entertained their hosts by setting off fireworks, which caused screams of fear and cries of wonder. The sailors also amazed the islanders when they rode horses, animals Tahitians had never seen.

After leaving gifts of livestock, Cook ordered his men to weigh anchor. He stopped at Moorea, a beautiful island he had never visited before.

A goat was stolen. Cook went into such an irrational rage that once again his officers were shocked. They reluctantly followed orders, and their men "burnt in all 20 Houses & 18 large War Canoes some of which row'd 100 & 120 Paddles."[10]

Such cruel punishment had been meted out to innocent people because they'd failed to return one goat! Cook had always been admired for his diplomacy that "rendered him highley respected & esteemed by all the Indians."[11] Midshipman Gilbert reported: "Neither tears nor entreaties could move Cook. He seem'd to be very rigid in the performance of His order . . . about such a trifle as a small goat. . . . I can't well account for Capt Cook's proceedings on this occasion; as they were so very different from his conduct in like cases in his former voyages."[12] Perhaps physical exhaustion and mental stress had unhinged Cook's judgment.

Mai Settled

After leaving Moorea in a shambles, Cook headed for Huahine, where he expected to establish a home for Mai. Cook had visited this island before, and Mai was anxious to settle there, believing that his wealth and splendor would bring him respect and power.

Cook paid fifteen axes and "some beads and trifles" for a plot of land along the shore. He ordered the ships' carpenters to build a house. Members of the crew planted a garden with vegetables and fruits. Furnished like an English cottage, with tables, chairs, dinnerware, and kitchen utensils, Mai felt equipped to dine there in grand style. In addition to the two New Zealand boys, he had hired several Tahitians to be servants. He had horses, pigs, goats, one rabbit, and a monkey to show off. And he placed his toys, tools, trinkets, gadgets, and guns on display to impress everyone—including the island chief, who was only ten years old.

Mai's new home was built near this shore.

Mai aroused envy, not admiration. Then something happened that made him live in fear. By flourishing a sword and using threats, Mai wormed a confession from a native who had taken a sextant. Cook punished the man by having his ears cut off—another example of the captain's extreme new form of vengeance. To get even with Mai, who had denounced him, the culprit threatened to burn Mai's house and kill him as soon as the ships had left.

When it was time to set sail the two New Zealand boys who worked for Mai were so upset that they swam out to the ships, weeping and pleading to stay with the expedition. They had to be forcibly carried to shore. "Mai took his leave . . . with a manly sorrow, until he came to Capt. Cook, when . . . he burst into tears."[13]

Before leaving the alluring South Sea Islands Cook spent several days at Raiatea, an island near Huahine. He seemed reluctant to quit the tropics, "having nothing to expect in the future but excess of cold, Hunger, and every kind of hardship and distress."[14] Again sailors deserted, but they were recovered before the ships sailed on December 7, 1777.[15]

Two men of the *Discovery* deserted because they could not bear to leave "engaging females." Once again Cook grabbed hostages. He seized a son, son-in-law, and daughter of the island chief, resolved to detain them until the deserters were brought back. Horrified, protesting native women slashed their heads until blood streamed down their faces and shoulders. This dismaying bloodletting ended after the deserters were found and when the chief's family was released. The defectors were put in irons until the ships sailed.

10 · SEARCH FOR A NORTHWEST PASSAGE

COOK SET HIS COURSE due north. He did not expect to sight land until he reached the American coast, where he would search for that fabulous Northwest Passage.

For several weeks the *Resolution* and *Discovery* sailed through uncharted seas. The day before Christmas Cook discovered a bare, uninhabited island, a bleak place to spend a holiday. However, turtle hunting made Christmas Island an exciting stopover. His men captured the live reptiles by swimming out in pairs, flipping the creatures onto their backs, grabbing their fins, then pulling them to shore.[1]

Hawaii Discovered

Cook sighted the Hawaiian island of Kauai the morning of January 19, 1778. Swarms of men, women, and children swam out to the *Resolution* and *Discovery*. Canoes seemed to be everywhere. The islanders were fascinated because they had never seen huge sailing ships before. Nor had they ever encountered light-skinned people with red, blond, or brown hair. Several were bold enough to venture on board, curious about aliens who had arrived out of the blue with unique

Masked paddlers

possessions. Mirrors astonished them. They thought china plates were made of wood. The Hawaiians were familiar with metal, which they had probably obtained from nails in timbers that had been washed ashore from wrecked ships. When they wondered what guns were, however, it was obvious they had never encountered European navigators before.

When Cook landed at Waimea Bay, the Hawaiians "all fell flat on their faces, and remained in that humble posture till . . . [he] made signs to them to rise."[2] This was the Hawaiians' way of honoring a high-ranking chief.

Cook and his officers were dumbfounded because the natives not only resembled Tahitians but also spoke a similar language—even though they were three thousand miles northwest of Tahiti! It was mind-boggling to realize that Tahitians must have migrated thousands of miles across the ocean in canoes, guided by the stars, wind directions, and ocean currents. Cook couldn't imagine how Pacific islanders could travel thousands of miles without a compass or a sextant.

Cook named these islands in the middle of nowhere the Sandwich Islands, in honor of the Earl of Sandwich, First Lord of the Admiralty.

With the discovery of Hawaii, Cook had visited the extremities of Polynesia: Hawaii in the north, New Zealand in the southwest, and Easter Island in the southeast. These islands stretched across 3,600 miles of ocean from north to

A Hawaiian wearing a gourd mask with a crest of ferns and dangling strings of bark

south and 5,000 miles from east to west. During this stopover Cook had landed on two Hawaiian islands: Kauai and Niihau. Although natives had informed Cook there were more islands in the Hawaiian group to investigate, he felt pressed to move on after a two-week stay. Discovering the Northwest Passage was the main reason for his expedition. On February 2, 1778, the *Resolution* and *Discovery* were again on their way.

The American Coast

Five weeks after leaving Hawaii, Cook was off the coast of present-day Oregon. Heavy gales with sleet, hail, and snow kept the ships from landing. The *Resolution* and the *Discovery* were forced to sail far from shore, thus making it impossible to map the coastline. But at least the ships were heading north.

Cook soon found a decent harbor at Nootka Sound, an inlet of Vancouver Island. Nootkans in canoes welcomed the

Nootka Sound

Racks of drying fish hang from the rafters of this house in Nootka Sound.

English by flinging feathers and red dust into the water, shaking rattles, shouting, and singing "something between a howl & a song." These "savages" were "bedaub'd with red & black Paint & Grease . . . their hair clott'd with dirt."[3]

Despite their fierce appearance, the Nootkans proved to be friendly. Jumping and gesticulating wildly, they shouted long welcoming speeches. Dressed in fur skins, wearing skillfully carved masks of human, bird, and animal faces, they danced and sang beautiful, melodious songs from their boats.

Trading was brisk. Knowing they were bound for the Arctic, sailors were eager for warm furs. Bear, beaver, sea-otter, and wolf skins were purchased. At first the price was a few copper coins or buttons, used as nose decorations. But the Nootkans proved to be clever traders whose prices went up day after day. They knew the value of iron, which they had probably obtained indirectly from Russian fur traders who dealt with other coastal tribes. Nootkans wanted metal in return for their wares. As a result, the crew broke up copper pans and teakettles. They gave away so many pewter plates that coconut shells intended as souvenirs from the South Seas had to be used as their dinner plates.

The Nootkans' strong sense of private property came as

a surprise. Cook complained that he had to pay for wood and water. Villagers even charged for grass the crew cut to feed their goats and sheep.

After four weeks at Nootka Sound the *Resolution* and *Discovery* headed north, hoping to find the Northwest Passage that would give them a shortcut to the Atlantic. Cook was in unknown waters, his main guides being copies of highly inaccurate Russian-made maps that depicted Alaska as an island. After sailing through storms that had the crew constantly working pumps to save the leaking *Resolution* from sinking, Cook steered north until he anchored at an inlet he called Sandwich Sound (Prince William Sound).

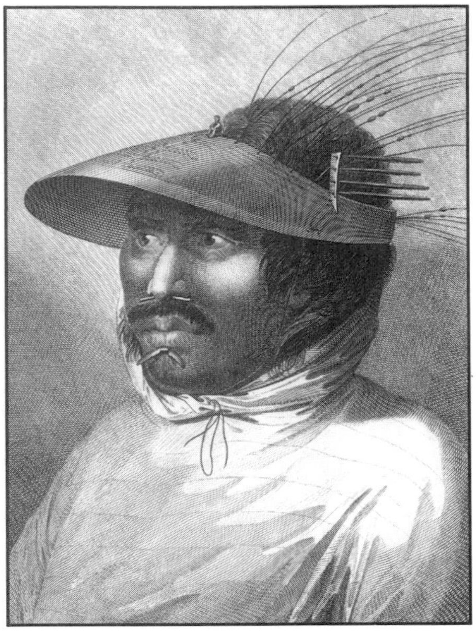

A man of Alaska and a woman of Price William Sound

One sailor shouted that he had seen a man with two mouths. Then others were astounded by the faces. "Both men, women, & children had a hole in their under lip, which was large enough to thrust their tongues thro, & it then lookd like a mouth."[4] It was "as if they had a double row of teeth in the under jaw."[5] Bones and strings of beads hung down through these holes and through other holes in their noses and ears. Painted faces made them seem even more monstrous. They were dressed in furs, with mittens made of bears' paws. Some wore hoods made of whales' intestines; others had high-crowned conical straw hats. These people were pleased to trade piles of sealskins for beads.[6]

Due to fog and the need to repair the *Resolution*, the expedition stayed eighteen days—enough time to realize that the natives weren't grotesque creatures but gentle, hardworking whale and seal hunters who were no more freakish than Englishmen wearing powdered wigs.

Tacking away from Prince William Sound, Cook was disheartened because the land veered west, not north. He became hopeful when he came upon an inlet on the Alaskan coast (now called Cook Inlet). Lieutenant Gore was so excited that he called it the "Gulf of Good Hope." However, when it proved to be a dead end, not a cross-continental waterway,

Prince William Sound

Gore changed his description to "Cape Lost Hope." A frustrated captain took the expedition out of the inlet, but not before his officers claimed the land for England by drinking wine to His Majesty's health and burying a bottle under some rocks. It contained a document with the date, the captain's name, and the names of the ships.

Following the coastline the ships continued to be approached by natives in kayaks who traded furs for a handful of nails, a few copper pennies, and any other things made of metal. As they moved along the Alaskan peninsula, Cook's men saw signs of European influence: people in cloth jackets and breeches, who doffed their hats and bowed like European peasants.

Russian fur trappers and traders had crossed from Siberia into Alaska and the Aleutian Islands. Furnishing Europe with foxes, ermines, and other warm, beautiful pelts proved so profitable that they frequently terrorized entire villages and forced the inhabitants to hunt for them. Sea-otter skins were the most precious furs of the northern Pacific. These were shipped to China and sold for enormous profits. The pelts were used to make luxurious coats for rich mandarins.

When the ships anchored at the Aleutian island of Unalaska, natives presented Captain Cook with a small, slotted wooden box. The gift was mistaken for a bird whistle, until it fell apart and two pieces of paper fell out with Russian script. Although Cook couldn't read them, he realized he was encroaching upon land occupied by Russians.

The Aleuts didn't offer skins for barter. The captain and his officers assumed that they were "fearful of selling us things because they had not permission [from their Russian masters] to do so."[7]

Although he spent four days at Unalaska, Cook did not encounter any Russians. He did not know that they were avoiding him because they believed the *Resolution* and *Discovery* were Japanese ships that had come to set up their own fur-trading station.

The Arctic Ocean

Cook then headed for the Bering Sea, which had become well known to geographers after Vitus Bering explored the area for Russia in 1728. The ships passed through the Bering Strait, which separates Asia from North America, then entered the Arctic Ocean, where a wall of ice twelve feet high blocked them. There was no way around. Cook had sailed as far north as he could. He had to turn back. But the captain wasn't about to quit the Arctic until his men hunted "sea horses," walruses that were swimming about and resting on floes. With his constant concern about the health of his men, he viewed these animals as a source of nourishing fresh meat. Hunting walrus was no great challenge, because these docile creatures could be shot at close range. The hard part was hoisting the one-ton carcasses on board.

The captain was capable of digesting any food he judged to be healthful. The rank smell and flavor of walrus meat repelled most of the men and made many sick to their stomachs. At first Cook insisted that everyone eat "sea horse" steaks and stews. Those who refused had to subsist on bread until "the discontents rose to such complaints & murmurings" that Cook backed down, and the crew returned to their diet of salted meat.[8]

Realizing that his ships might be imprisoned in ice if he did not hurry away from the northern Pacific, Cook announced—much to the joy of the crew—that his ships would spend the winter in Hawaii and return north the fol-

Shooting walruses for food

lowing summer, to continue his search for the Northwest Passage.

The *Resolution* and *Discovery* groped southeast along the Siberian Arctic coast. After an island stopover (at a place called St. Lawrence Island by the Russians) they reached American shores just east of present-day Nome and coasted along Norton Sound. The men were allowed to land in order to pick berries and cut spruce for making beer.

On October 2, 1778, the ships reached Unalaska in the Aleutians (now part of the state of Alaska). Once again the leaking *Resolution* had to be fixed, while the *Discovery* needed overhauling. The stopover was delightful. Fishing was fantastic, for the waters teemed with halibut. Cook declared that "the Native inhabitants . . . are the most peaceable inoffensive people I ever met with, and as to honisty they might serve as a pattern to the most civilized nation upon earth."[9] He failed to realize that the people he so admired were enslaved. Under the Russian yoke, they were forbidden to carry arms, and they would have been killed if they took anything from their foreign masters.

An Aleut brought Cook a gift of two fish pies and an incomprehensible message in Russian. Cook was anxious to let the Russians know "we were English, Friends and Allies."[10] Marine Corporal John Ledyard, from Connecticut, volunteered to wander into the wilderness until he located Russian traders. (He was especially eager, convinced that West Coast fur trading could benefit American merchant ships.) Cook instructed him to report back in a week. Ledyard carried no weapons. Bread and a flask of rum were his only provisions.

The first night Ledyard slept with an Aleut family who lived in a small, sunk-in-the-ground hut. The next day Ledyard was led to a cove, where a kayak "with holes to accommodate two sitters" picked him up. Ledyard was "stowed away" flat on his back. After about an hour the

Paddling sealskin kayaks

native canoe struck a beach. Then he was pulled out of the kayak by two Russians and brought to a trading station, where a small band of Russians lived in one dwelling with their servants. Although verbal communication was hopeless, Ledyard managed to charm his hosts, who stripped off his wet British clothes and dressed him "like one of themselves," in a blue silk shirt, fur cap, boots, and gown. They insisted he enjoy a steam bath in a special sauna hut. When the heat made him faint, they revived him with cold water, but he was in no condition to face a breakfast consisting of whale, walrus, and smoked bear. The smells made him feel so sick that he requested salmon, which he ate with his own biscuits.[11]

Three Russians were delighted to return with Ledyard. He had told them about the great British navigator, Captain Cook, and they wanted to meet him. Since there was no interpreter, the men communicated using signs and nods. Cook wanted maps, but his visitors couldn't help him. Several days later, Governor Ismyloff, who was chief of the Russian settlement, arrived with a map of the Russian discoveries in America. In appreciation, Cook gave Ismyloff a quadrant, a valuable instrument for finding latitude, and ordered one of his officers to explain its use.

Winter was setting in. Cook was irritated because he was delayed three weeks, while carpenters continued to repair the ships. The crew, however, relaxed and enjoyed themselves. They socialized with families living in a Russian settlement that was only fifteen miles away. The Russians welcomed the company of other Europeans to their desolate fur-trading outpost.

On October 26, 1778, the *Resolution* and *Discovery* set sail again and headed for Hawaii. Captain Cook charted the first detailed map of the American northwest coast and traced in considerable detail both the Asian shores and American shores of the Bering Strait.

Cook was undoubtedly frustrated and dejected because he had failed to find the Northwest Passage. After years at sea he must have felt disheartened, for the Southern Continent did not exist, and a waterway crossing America had not been found. He did not realize his importance as a discoverer of tremendous areas of the Pacific Ocean. Its sea space covers one-third of the earth, an area greater than all the land in the world.

11 · CAPTAIN COOK, HAWAIIAN "GOD"

AFTER THE BRUTAL winter weather, everyone looked forward to warm sunshine, good food, and willing women. One month after heading away from the chattering cold of the northwest, Cook's men sighted Maui, a Hawaiian island they had not visited before. (The ships had drifted too far east to return to Kauai and Niihau.)[1] Jagged volcanic lava rocks covered its shores and steep cliffs jutted out over the ocean. Finding a decent harbor seemed futile. Anyway, Cook was in no hurry to land, because he could buy provisions from Hawaiians who paddled out to the ships. He ordered the *Resolution* and *Discovery* to cruise slowly along the coast of Maui, then along the island of Hawaii.

The men were at sea, yet close to shore for seven weeks. Being confined to the ships was a torment. Only authorized officers were permitted to trade with the Hawaiians who arrived in canoes. No females were allowed because some of the seamen had venereal diseases, and Cook felt morally obligated to prevent them from infecting native women.[2]

Confinement at sea became more exasperating when Cook concocted a new drink: "beer" made from quantities of sugar cane he had purchased from visiting traders. Cook considered it "palatable and wholesome," but the crew found it "not fit for human beings." In a vile mood, and describing his men as a "Mutinous crew" who would not even taste his most recent healthful potion, Cook issued orders that "no grog [strong liquor] should be served in either Ship."[3]

No drinking; no trading; no land excursions; no women! Away from England for two and a half years! How tantalizing to see but not touch the land of a tropical paradise! The men were so disgruntled that a few days before Christmas Cook gave in. Grog was served, and girls were allowed on board—but only for those men with a clean bill of health.

Storms and squalls caused the ships to separate. They lost contact with each other for thirteen days. After that upsetting situation, Captain Cook was happy to find a suitable harbor. On January 17, 1779, he reached Kealakekua Bay on the island of Hawaii.

Cook was astounded by its enormous population—more people than he had seen anywhere else in the Pacific. "The

Kealakekua Bay

A Hawaiian woman

Ships very much *Crouded* with Indians and surrounded by a multitude of Canoes . . . Besides those in the Canoes all the Shore of the bay was covered with people and hundreds were swimming about the Ships like shoals of fish . . . a number of men upon pieces of Plank [surfboards]."[4]

The *Discovery* had so many islanders hanging on its side that she tipped "considerably." The Hawaiians were "so thick on the Decks, that there was no moving."[5] These people had never encountered European men. Nor had they ever seen such huge ships. Cook had to request the help of two chiefs who had come aboard to visit. They cleared the decks by shooing some back to their canoes and by tossing others overboard so they could swim to shore.

There was one special, spectacular-looking guest, the holy high priest Koa. He came aboard dressed in a magnificent cap and mantle made of birds' feathers. While uttering

A Hawaiian dancer holding a feathered rattle

lengthy incantations, he draped a red cloth around Cook's shoulders and placed hogs and fruits at the captain's feet. During his prayers he addressed Cook as "Lono."

Lono was the Hawaiian god of prosperity and peace. Makahiki, a sacred season that lasted from October to January, was dedicated to this deity. During that time warfare was forbidden, hard work stopped, and feasts with religious celebrations took place. Parades featured white banners that signified Lono's holiness. Paying taxes in the form of provisions (to benefit priests) was the only unpleasant part of this holiday season.

Lono was envisioned as a white god fated to arrive on a magical floating island during the holiday of Makahiki. Behold Cook, the imposing alien dressed in exotic costume! He had come to them during the sacred season in time for the great ceremonies in his honor. His ships' huge sails were construed to be long staffs bearing Lono's divine white banners. As was prophesied, the revered god had returned. Without doubt, Cook was Lono!

When Cook landed on the beach, he was greeted by men holding wands tipped with dog hair. They kept repeating the word "Lono," his new name. When the captain passed through a village, all the natives threw themselves to the ground face-down and didn't get up until he had passed. During his first visit to Hawaii, he had been revered as a great chief. At this time, however, he was being worshiped as a god.

Hawaiians led Cook, Lieutenant King, and the astronomer Bayly to the top of a pile of stones that also included twenty human skulls. Then the group entered an area near the beach that contained a semicircle of twelve wooden images. Priest Koa wrapped a huge amount of red cloth around Cook, gave him a hog to hold, and led him in front of each image. Koa prostrated himself before the center image, kissed it, and instructed Cook to do so, too.

The captain cooperated. He allowed himself to be rubbed with coconut that had been saturated with saliva, drank kava from chewed-up roots, and permitted mouthfuls of minced pig to be transferred from a chief's mouth to his own. How typical of Cook, who was curious about customs and ever anxious to please and befriend his hosts! He did admit, however, that he found the pig meat hard to swallow, but he enjoyed playing the role of Lono.

During Cook's stay an observatory and camp were set up in a sweet-potato field, which was made *taboo* (off limits), so that commoners could not visit. It was declared sacred ground—too sacred from the crew's point of view, because women were banned. Priests would kill any female caught there.

To honor Lono, Hawaii's King Kalaniopuu arrived from Maui in a magnificent, sixty-foot-long canoe. Two other great canoes accompanied him. One was occupied by chant-

A ceremony honoring Cook as the god Lono

ing chiefs escorting "the busts of what we supposed [were] their Gods made of basket work, variously covered with red, black, white, & Yellow feathers."[6] The other was stacked with mounds of yams, hogs, and other foodstuffs.

King Kalaniopuu boarded the *Resolution* to inspect Lono's sacred floating island, with its many compartments and mysterious implements. Cook was surprised to find that Kalaniopuu was one of the chiefs who had visited him off the coast of Maui eight weeks before. At that time Cook had not been aware of his power and importance.

Kalaniopuu and his retinue escorted the captain to shore and entered the expedition's encampment. Formal ceremonies took place in the astronomer's tent. "The King got up & threw in a graceful manner on the Captain's Shoulders the Cloak he himself wore, & put a feather Cap upon his head, & a very handsom fly flap in his hand: besides which he laid down at the Captains feet 5 or 6 Cloaks more, all very beautiful."[7] Then a procession of priests appeared, bearing additional gifts of hogs, bananas, and sweet potatoes. During

Islanders went out to see Cook's ships.

these ceremonies, commoners' heads touched the ground and no canoes were allowed in the bay.

Whenever Cook went for a stroll a priest preceded him, heralding the approach of the divine Lono. "Every Body Layed down flat before him as he passed."[8] Ritual honors surrounded Cook wherever he walked. A train of praying priests collected pigs and other produce from commoners for their visiting god—and for themselves.

Wrestling and boxing matches were staged in Cook's honor. Although invited to participate, the Englishmen had learned their lesson when they were beaten at these sports at the Friendly Islands. To impress their hosts, the crew set off fireworks—celestial lights that radiated to the heavens as though divinely ordered.

People were so peaceable that unarmed crew members took excursions into the countryside, guided and guarded by islanders. Carpenters collecting timber were aided by Hawaiians, who carried heavy loads for them.

The need for firewood was crucial before the ships could leave. Sailors not only took the fence of a sacred *heiau* (ceremonial area) but also carried away carved images of several gods. Lieutenant King was sent to apologize to the priest Kao, who didn't seem disturbed and merely asked that one image clothed in wrappings be returned.

Lieutenant James King's manners were so pleasing that Kalaniopuu and Koa wanted him to stay. They told him that they would hide him in the hills until the ships had gone and make him a "great man." King was flattered and amused. He wrote that they wanted him as "a Curious play thing"—just as Banks had wanted a Pacific islander to amuse his friends. When told about it, Cook was diplomatic, and "to avoid giving a positive refusal" he said that perhaps Lieutenant King could stay another time, not now.[9]

The death of an old seaman named William Watman may have seemed unsettling to natives who worshiped Cook as a god. This proved that Lono's servants were mortals—a fact that may have diminished their esteem for Cook. Nevertheless, chiefs allowed Watman to be buried in a sacred area, and for three nights they chanted prayers and threw killed hogs on his grave.

On February 4, 1779, the ships unmoored and sailed away, much to the relief of King Kalaniopuu and the priest Koa, because they were concerned about the quantities of food they felt obligated to supply to their god.

12 · THE KILLING OF CAPTAIN COOK

THE SHIPS had barely reached the open sea when a sudden storm with furious gales ripped sails and broke the *Resolution*'s mainmast. Cook realized he had to turn back. One week later, on February 11, 1779, the *Resolution* and *Discovery* anchored once again in Kealakekua Bay.

The men were surprised that they weren't greeted by joyous Hawaiians. There were no cheering, shouting people; no processions by chiefs and priests who had welcomed them before. The bay was deserted, with only a few canoes close to shore.

When Cook landed, no one bowed, their heads on the ground. And when he set up tents at his old headquarters, the islanders seemed vexed and resentful. The sacred Makahiki season celebrating Lono the god had ended on February 4, on the very day Cook had left them. Why had he returned *after* his sacred holiday? Why would a god's ship need to be repaired? Many now suspected that Cook was not Lono, the Divine One.

When King Kalaniopuu visited the *Resolution*, he was visibly upset because Cook had returned. Lono was not supposed to come back for one year. According to Hawaiian religious belief, another god, Ku, became the chief object of

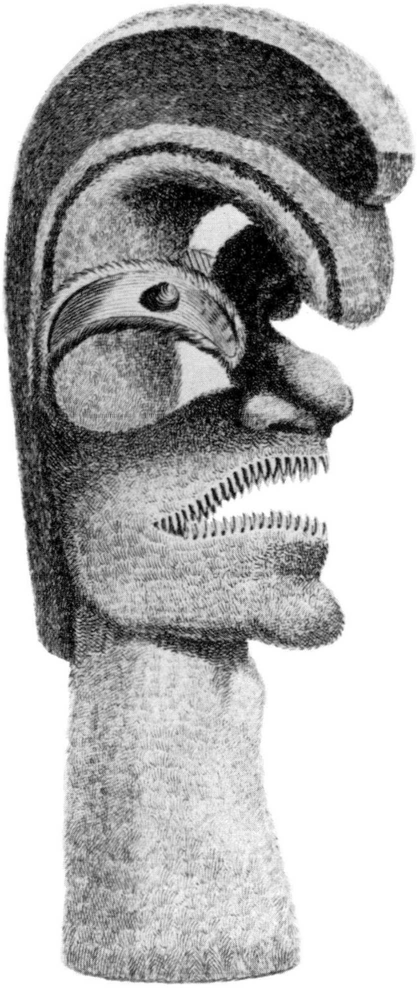

Ku, Hawaiian god of war

worship after Lono's departure. And the divine Ku was the king's legendary ancestor! Without realizing it, Cook as Lono seemed to be challenging Ku's power—thus causing fear and anxiety. Moreover, people had donated so much food to Lono that additional offerings of pigs and fruits would impose hardship.

After the king's visit the decks were jammed with islanders who were so rude and unruly that both Cook and Clerke had them thrown off their ships. Natives were especially nasty when a party of sailors, aided by other natives, were collecting casks of water. First some chiefs ordered the Hawaiian helpers to leave. Then a mob threatened to throw stones at the sailors.

When he heard about this, Cook was overcome by fury. He ordered Lieutenant King "that on the first appearance of throwing stones or behaving insolently, to fire ball at the offenders."[1] Sentries were directed to load *ball* not *shot*! Shot injures. *Ball kills*! This was an astonishing directive from Captain Cook, who had always tried to avoid violence, a man many of the crew admired because he was "ever too tender of the Lives of Indians."[2]

Everyone was on edge. A Hawaiian caught trying to grab a pair of tongs was harshly punished with forty lashes.

Then, while Clerke was entertaining Chief Pareea on the *Discovery*, one of the chief's attendants seized the tongs, dived overboard, and paddled to shore using the chief's canoe. A boatload of sailors chased him and recovered the tongs, but the islander got away. When Chief Pareea was rowed to shore on one of the *Discovery*'s boats, he was enraged because his own canoe had been seized and was being held by sailors.

A fight broke out. A seaman conked Pareea on the head with an oar. Angry Hawaiians attacked by throwing stones and wielding clubs. Then they started to rip bolts and other iron parts from the *Discovery*'s boat. Chief Pareea stopped them because he still feared that Cook might be a god. After receiving "many hard thumps [the men] were glad to get their Boats off with half the Oars broke, lost."[3]

When Cook heard about this incident he was determined to lash out against the Hawaiians to show his superior power. "I am afraid," he said, "that these people will oblige me to use some violent measures; for they must not be left to imagine that they have gained an advantage over us."[4]

At night the *Discovery*'s large cutter was taken—a very serious matter, because this was the only large boat the *Discovery* had. At daybreak, as soon as Clerke heard about the loss, he went to the *Resolution* to inform Cook. Cook ordered Clerke to blockade the bay so that no native canoes could leave.

Taking hostages had been effective so many times that Cook resolved to hold King Kalaniopuu captive until the cutter was returned. He landed with an armed party of one officer and nine marines. Muskets were loaded with ball. Cook's own double-barreled gun had both shot and ball. The king, who knew nothing about the cutter, was asleep in his home. When awakened by Lieutenant Phillips, he readily agreed to go to the *Resolution* with Cook.

Accompanied by two lively young sons who always enjoyed visiting the *Resolution*, the physically feeble king followed Cook and his marines. Near the waterside one of the king's wives stopped him. She wept and begged him not to board Cook's ship. Two chiefs who were with her forced Kalaniopuu to sit down. "The old Man now appear'd dejected and frighten'd."[5]

Hundreds of Hawaiians seemed to appear from nowhere, armed with stones, spears, and daggers. Realizing that it would be impossible to compel the king to proceed unless his men opened fire on the Hawaiians, Cook abandoned his plan to make him a hostage.

It was too late to halt the violence. Before Cook could leave, two natives arrived from the other side of the bay with

Two versions of the killing of Captain Cook, by painters who were not eyewitnesses but who heard the stories from crew members

news that one of their high-ranking chiefs had been shot—the result of Cook's order to prevent any canoe from pulling out.

This news spread like wildfire and provoked further fury. With a dagger in one hand and a stone in the other, one of the Hawaiians threatened Cook. Cook fired at his assailant, who wasn't injured. As a result of Cook's action, however, the alarmed crowd became enraged. Fierce fighting broke out. Hawaiians attacked marines with clubs, spears, and daggers. Sailors waiting in the boats and marines on shore shot into the crowd. Cook fired again and killed a man. He ordered the marines to shoot and "take to the boats."[6]

Cook was waving the boats in when he was hit from behind with a club. While staggering from the blow, he was stabbed in the back. Cook fell face-down in the water. He was held underwater and stabbed again and again.

When the captain fell "all was confusion & the Marines plunged into the Water & made for the Boats."[7] Leaving Cook and four marines dead, they were hastily rowed to their ships.

The news of Cook's death stunned the crew: "They cryed out with Tears in the Eyes that they had lost their Father!"[8]

Charles Clerke now assumed overall command of the expedition. He moved to the *Resolution* and chose the Virginian, Lieutenant John Gore, to command the *Discovery*.

Six marines were still on land guarding the *Resolution*'s repaired mast. Aided by the fire of the *Discovery*'s cannon, a party led by Lieutenant King landed, forced stone-throwing Hawaiians to retreat, rescued the men, and recovered the mast.

The next night Captain Clerke sent Lieutenant King to demand Cook's body. As a precaution, King's boat did not land but stayed offshore, "near enough to hold conversation." Chief Koa swam out and "promis'd we should have the body of Captain Cook tomorrow but that it was carried too far up the Country to be brought down tonight."[9]

The next morning Koa made several trips in a small canoe flying a white flag of truce (a sign of peace probably learned from the crew). He assured the officers that Cook's remains would be returned.

At night a priest, "a friend of Mr. Kings came on board and brought with him a large piece of Flesh . . . part of the Corpse of our late unfortunate Captain, it was clearly part of the Thigh." The priest informed them that the rest of the flesh had been burned at different places for "some peculiar ceremony," adding that "the Bones which were all that now remain'd were in the possession of King Kalaniopuu."[10]

The sight was so revolting that revenge was on everyone's mind. Clerke prevented his men from attacking. He was intent upon receiving the rest of Cook's remains and the bodies of the fallen marines. He also realized that he could not set sail until the ships had taken on a supply of water.

The men could hear moaning and screeching by people who were probably burying their dead. They also saw fires punctuating the land: probably religious offerings of the bones and flesh of Cook and the four dead marines.

It was maddening to be the butt of such insults. One insolent islander paddled around, wearing Captain Cook's hat, while people on shore hooted and laughed. Others defiantly sported clothing that had belonged to the dead marines. When a watering party came ashore the men were pelted with stones.

It was impossible to contain the overwhelming passion for revenge. Men sent to collect water set a town on fire. They destroyed at least fifty homes and a number of sacred buildings. They shot Hawaiians and cut off the heads of two victims as grisly trophies, which they brought back to the ships.

After this violence, the Hawaiians begged for peace. They carried white flags and gifts of food to the beach. Watering parties were no longer molested, and priests asked if their old friendships with the officers could be resumed. King Kalaniopuu sent a message that he was "very desirous of Peace."[11] Clerke retorted that friendly relations could be restored only after the rest of Captain Cook's body was returned.

The afternoon of February 20, six days after the disaster, the remains of Captain Cook were delivered, "very decently wrapped up in a large quantity of fine new Cloth." The bundle contained "bones with some flesh upon them which had the marks of fire."[12]

The dismemberment of Cook had been an act of respect, not hate. As with any great chief, the captain's bones were venerated as sacred relics. His flesh had been burned as a sacrifice to the Hawaiian gods.[13]

Clerke asked for the return of the marines' bodies. A priest explained that their corpses had also been dismembered and distributed among various chiefs in different parts of the island. It would be impossible to locate the remains.

Men suffered in deep mourning. Both ships hoisted their pennants at half staff, tolled bells, and fired ten cannon shots while they committed the bones of Captain Cook to the deep.

Chief Kanina, one of the islanders killed during the struggle

13 · HOMEWARD BOUND

CLERKE COULD HAVE ordered the ships to head for England, but, following Cook's plan, he was intent upon searching once again for the elusive Northwest Passage.

As the ships sailed north, sleet, snow, and ice covered the ropes and sails. Men suffered from frostbite, and their new commander, Charles Clerke, was dying. He had tuberculosis, a sickness that he'd developed shortly after the third expedition began.

On April 29, 1779, six weeks after leaving Hawaii, the ships reached Kamchatka, in Siberia. Clerke wanted the Russians to supply him with fresh provisions. He also needed an extended stay to repair his battered, leaking ships. Russian officials were reluctant to offer assistance until Major Behm, the governor of Kamchatka, arrived and authorized them to do so. The major greeted them graciously, not only because they had been led by the famous navigator Captain James Cook, but also because any European company in this bleak Siberian outpost was cause for fine hospitality.

The major provided flour, fish, beef, and tobacco for the ships and supplied servants, housing, and dog sleds for the officers. Madame Behm gave an elegant party, attended by "Ladies dress'd out in the Silk Cloaks, lined with very val-

The *Resolution* heads for home.

Gore, King, and Webber used dogsleds of this type at Kamchatka.

uable & different colourd furs, which had a most rich appearance."[1] It was amazing to find luxury in such a dreary country.

When the ailing Clerke learned that Behm expected to leave for St. Petersburg, he entrusted him with Captain Cook's journals and charts. These documents and an up-to-date report were to be sent on from Russia to the Admiralty in England. They would arrive before the expedition returned. Clerke wished to guarantee that these valuable papers would not be lost at sea, in case of shipwreck.

On June 16, when the *Resolution* and *Discovery* prepared to leave the harbor, people lined the streets, singing to them. Soldiers marched down to the water's edge and shouted three cheers as a farewell tribute.

Once again the ships sailed through fog in freezing weather. Three weeks after they had passed through the Bering Strait they were stopped by a wall of ice that rose twenty feet out of the water. Clerke persisted in directing the ships from one continent to the other until he concluded that the sea was so choked with ice that "a [northwest] passage . . . is totally out of the question."[2]

Disheartened, and desperately ill, Clerke headed the ships back to Kamchatka. He died on August 22, 1779, several days before the ships docked. This fine, able officer was buried under a tree near the harbor. John Gore took command of the *Resolution*, and Lieutenant James King took Gore's place as commander of the *Discovery*.

Seven weeks passed before the ships' damaged rudders, battered bows, and ripped sails were repaired. The officers decided to return home by way of the Cape of Good Hope. The journey south was "the most disagreeable . . . having continual gale of wind, with very Severe Squalls, Thunder, Lightning, and Rain, and an extraordinary high sea."[3] The ships passed Iwo Jima, whose active volcano pelted them with pea-sized pumice stones and covered the decks with ashes and mud. Later they were nearly wrecked on a shoal in the China Sea.

On December 4, 1779, the ships anchored off Macao, a Portuguese colony near Canton, China. Having heard no news from England for three years, all were anxious to learn about conditions in Europe. It was upsetting to find out that France and England were at war, and terribly shocking to hear that colonists in America were also battling the British. Arming the *Resolution* and *Discovery* in case of attack by French and American ships seemed urgent. Gore bought six additional cannon, reinforced the railings, and built up the ships' sides to protect the gunners.

During a visit to Canton, King learned news that boosted everyone's spirits. Benjamin Franklin had drafted orders to commanders of American ships. They were not to prevent the expedition from returning to England, because "the most celebrated Navigator and Discoverer Captain Cook" had increased geographical information and "Science of other kinds . . . to the Benefit of Mankind in general."[4] Although the expedition's captains didn't know it at the time, the French also perceived the third expedition to be such an important scientific mission that the king of France had ordered his navy not to attack. And Spain, having joined the war against England, had declared the *Resolution* and *Discovery* to be neutral, not to be molested. Like spaceships heading for the moon, Cook's sailing vessels had worldwide significance because they were revealing mysteries about the planet Earth. Their mission was meaningful for all nations.

At Macao and Canton the furs that the crew had collected and used for warm bedding and clothing were sold to the Chinese at exorbitant prices. Many of the sailors talked about going back to the northern Pacific as fur traders, where they could exchange trinkets for valuable pelts. Lured by the prospect of riches, two of the *Resolution*'s crew deserted.

After six weeks at Macao, the expedition sailed for the Cape of Good Hope, where they remained one month because the ships needed repairs before heading for England. Contrary winds forced them north of the English Channel. On August 22, 1780, they anchored at the Orkney Islands, northeast of Scotland. James King made his way to London with documents about the expedition. Most of the news he conveyed had been known for nine months, through the journals and charts Clerke had sent on from Siberia by way of Russia.

On October 4, 1780, the ships finally arrived in London. The voyage had lasted four years, two months, and twenty-two days. During that time fifteen men had died: seven from sickness, three through accidents, and five killed at Kealakekua Bay. No man had died from scurvy. The men were home at last, but home without Captain Cook, "their father . . . whose great Qualities they venerated almost to adoration."[5]

Captain Cook's achievements were acclaimed throughout

Europe. He was justifiably hailed as one of history's greatest navigators. As a result of his accurate charts and his proof that proper diet prevents scurvy, ships and crews were able to travel to the other side of the globe with safety. He had opened the way to commerce and colonization in untapped parts of the world.

By studying and describing various peoples and cultures of the Pacific, Cook replaced fiction with fact. He did not find monsters, giants, and mindless savages. Instead, there were natives in faraway places who were beautiful, intelligent, and admirable in many of their ways.

A Nootkan woman, wearing a waterproof basket hat, decorated with whales

Before Cook left for his final voyage, Joseph Banks persuaded him to sit for this portrait by Nathaniel Dance.

After Cook's voyages, the lives of Pacific peoples were drastically transformed. Their countries were occupied and dominated by strangers who had never been invited to their shores. Not only were their lands commercially exploited, but their cultural values were criticized. Western beliefs, laws, and life-styles were adopted, or imposed upon them. Made to feel inferior because they lacked the industrial accomplishments of Europeans, they were taught to admire and desire material possessions, including guns. They became susceptible to "improvement" dictated by foreigners, who were not concerned about people's cultural heritage, or about their territorial rights.

Captain Cook's explorations were tremendously influential upon the English, who subsequently colonized and developed New Zealand and Australia. His journals excited British and American interest in the fur trade and in the occupation of the North American Pacific Coast. By discovering Hawaii he provided an ideal stop-over for whalers and merchant ships. As a vital supply station between the Orient and the western world, Hawaii was to become a strategically and commercially valuable part of the United States.

The remarkable voyages of Captain Cook cleared clouds of myth and mystery that hung over the Pacific, from the Antarctic to the Arctic. Cook destroyed beliefs in an idyllic Southern Continent and in a fantastic Northwest Passage. By charting vast areas of the world's largest ocean, he replaced old maps inspired by imagination with maps drawn through observation. Truth, not legend, shaped the new geography that this great explorer gave to the world.

NOTES

1 · An Unknown Continent

1. Ptolemy, the "father of geography" who lived during the second century, had pronounced this falsehood as fact. His teachings were accepted as truths for hundreds of years and were respected by geographers throughout most of the eighteenth century.
2. J. C. Beaglehole, *The Exploration of the Pacific*, 192–193. Beaglehole states that Dalrymple affirmed that a southern continent was necessary "for the Earth's motion" and that the space unknown in the Pacific Ocean from the equator to 50° S must be nearly all land.
3. *The Journals of Captain James Cook* I, 513.
4. *Ibid.* I, 512 (Letter to Council. Dec. 18, 1767).
5. J. C. Beaglehole, *The Life of Captain James Cook*, 89.
6. Tahiti had been sighted some 150 years earlier by the Portuguese navigator Quiros. Wallis discovered it June 18, 1767.
7. *The Journals of Captain James Cook* I, 620.
8. *Ibid.* I, 620.
9. *Ibid.* I, cclxxxi.
10. *Ibid.* I, Appendix II, 519, *Transactions of the Royal Society relative to sending out people to Observe the transit of Venus in 1769.*

2 · Voyage to Tahiti

1. *The Journals of Captain James Cook* I, 16.
2. On board Banks even rummaged through fresh fodder delivered for the ship's animals, and managed to find more new varieties of plants.
3. Bernard Smith, *European Vision and the South Pacific*, 34, n. Captain Byron was the poet's grandfather. An account of the captain's travels was used in Lord Byron's poem *Don Juan*.

4. Despite Banks's careful measurements, the giant story persisted. People love preposterous tales and want to believe them. Wasn't it possible that Banks had encountered just one tribe and failed to meet the "enormous goblins" that Captain Byron had described? Even after Cook's voyage ended, stories about Patagonian giants were printed and enhanced with illustrations.
5. "Indian" was a term used to describe any inhabitant who was not European, African, or Asian.
6. *The Journals of Captain James Cook* I, 44.
7. These had been handed to Banks, not to him, because Dalrymple disdained him.
8. *The Journals of Captain James Cook* I, 68. This statement was so offensive to Dalrymple that his disdain for Cook turned to bitter hatred of him.

3 · PACIFIC PARADISE

1. *The Journals of Captain James Cook* I, 76.
2. Matavai Bay is the Tahitian name. Captain Wallis of the *Dolphin* called it Port Royal.
3. Joseph Banks, *The Endeavour Journal of Joseph Banks* I, 252.
4. *The Journals of Captain James Cook* I, 77.
5. *Ibid.* I, 78.
6. *Ibid.* I, 80.
7. *Ibid.* I, 96, n.
8. *Ibid.* I, 87.
9. Joseph Banks, *The Endeavour Journal* I, 330.
10. Bernard Smith, 42.
11. Native girls made fun of Captain Cook because he was not lured by their charms. However, Cook was no prude. He didn't condemn sexual freedom. He refused to judge Tahitians by European moral standards. Cook condoned the lovemaking as "more from custom than Lewdness." J. C. Beaglehole, *The Life of Captain James Cook*, 122.
12. Banks I, Appendix, 334.
13. *Ibid.* I, 331.
14. *Ibid.* I, Appendix, 347.
15. *Ibid.* I, 289.
16. *The Journals of Captain James Cook* I, 86.
17. *Ibid.* I, 123.
18. *Ibid.* I, 127.
19. *Ibid.* I, 127.
20. Banks I, 312–313. This comment was probably made in jest. Banks did *not* equate natives with animals.
21. This group included Tahiti, Huahine, Ataha, and Raiatea. Cook had seen seventeen islands. According to Tupia, there were 130 in the vicinity.

4 · Cannibals and Goblins

1. Joseph Banks, *The Endeavour Journal* II, 399.
2. Te Horeta, a Maori chief, described the *Endeavour* invasion, having heard about it from his father. See J. C. Beaglehole, *The Life of Captain James Cook*, 206.
3. *The Journals of Captain James Cook* I, 172.
4. The original discoverers and settlers were Polynesians who arrived, probably from Tahiti, between A.D. 750 and 780.
5. Banks II, 417.
6. *The Journals of Captain James Cook* I, 236–237.
7. Banks II, 31.
8. *The Journals of Captain James Cook* I, 236, n.

5 · A Unique Land

1. Lynne Withey, *Voyages of Discovery*, 151.
2. *The Journals of Captain James Cook* I, 325.
3. *Ibid.* I, 395–396.
4. *Ibid.* I, 312.
5. Joseph Banks, *The Endeavour Journal* II, 116.
6. *The Journals of Captain James Cook* I, 399.
7. Banks II, 55.
8. For fifteen years Britain did nothing about sending settlers to Australia. The loss of the American colonies was a major cause for colonizing Australia. Convicts who had formerly been shipped to America were shipped to Australia. Loyalists from the American colonies also found asylum there.
9. Banks II, 79.
10. *Ibid.* II, 84.
11. *The Journals of Captain James Cook* I, 355, n.
12. Banks II, 180.
13. *Ibid.* II, 7.
14. *The Journals of Captain James Cook* I, 74.
15. *Ibid.* II, 94, n.3.
16. *Ibid.* I, 444–445.
17. Cook noted that New Guinea was not connected to Australia, thus exploding another myth held by geographers.

6 · "Mr. Banks's Trip"

1. *The Journals of Captain James Cook* I, Appendix, Newspaper accounts, 642–655.
2. Joseph Banks, *The Endeavour Journal* I, Introduction, 55.

3. *The Journals of Captain James Cook* I, Appendix VII, Newspaper Extracts, 642–655.
4. Cook, who was so careful about describing daily events while away, was private about his family life. Little is known about his role as husband and father. There are no letters to his wife. These may have been destroyed by her as too personal for others to see.
5. *The Journals of Captain James Cook* II, Intro. XXX.

7 · A Second Quest for Continent

1. *The Journals of Captain James Cook* II, 75, n.
2. Cape Circumcision is a tiny island.
3. *The Journals of Captain James Cook* II, 166.
4. *Ibid.* II, 293.
5. *Ibid.* II, 333, n.
6. *Ibid.* II, 322.
7. *Ibid.* II, 353. Cook referred to an anonymous author of *Roggewein's Voyage*, 353, n.
8. *Ibid.* II, Clerke's Log, 373–374.
9. *Ibid.* II, 404.
10. Polynesia, meaning "many islands," forms a triangle defined by Hawaii above the equator, New Zealand to the south, and Easter Island far to the east.

    Melanesia, meaning "black islands," is located between the equator and the Tropic of Capricorn. It encompasses New Guinea, the Solomon Islands, New Hebrides, New Caledonia, and the Fijis.
11. *The Journals of Captain James Cook* II, 621.
12. *Ibid.* II, 638.
13. *Ibid.* II, 643. The continent of Antarctica was not officially discovered until 1820. Some scholars attribute the discovery to a whaler; others to British or Soviet explorers. (John Wilford, *Mapmakers*, 267.)
14. *Ibid.* II, 647: "My people were yet healthy and would cheerfully have gone wherever I had thought them proper to lead them, but I dreaded the Scurvy."

8 · Interlude in England

1. Jean Jacques Rousseau's *Discourse on Inequality*, published in 1755, argued that savages were free, happy, and virtuous. Civilization was the corrupting influence. After Cook's first expedition, Tahiti was romanticized by Europeans as the home of the noble savage.
2. *Omai, or a Trip Round the World* was a popular play during the 1780s. In the play, Queen Purea, a rival for power, fails in her attempt to kill Mai. Mai is crowned king.
3. *The Journals of Captain James Cook* II, 669 (Cook to Walker, Aug. 19, 1775).
4. In 1497 John Cabot made the first attempt to find the passage for England. When he landed in North America he thought he had reached Asia. In 1498 he set out again to sail through the Northwest Passage but was lost at sea.

5. There was to be a double-pronged attempt. Richard Pickersgill, who had sailed with Cook on his first and second voyages, was to look for an entrance to the waterway from the Atlantic side, while Cook probed inlets of the North Pacific. The Admiralty hoped both expeditions would meet somewhere in the Arctic. When Pickersgill's ship was stopped by ice, he turned back and never probed the eastern coast.
6. *The Journals of Captain James Cook* III, The Instructions, ccxx–ccxxiv.

9 · Mai Brought Home

1. *The Journals of Captain James Cook* III, 14.
2. On the *Resolution*: William Ewin, boatswain from Pennsylvania; Benjamin Whitton, carpenter's mate, from Massachusetts; John Gore, first lieutenant, from Virginia; George Steward, sailor from South Carolina; John Ledyard, marine corporal from Connecticut.

   On the *Discovery*: Nathaniel Portlock, sailor, from "America"; Simon Woodruff, sailor, from Connecticut.

   There were also Americans on the first and second expeditions, but the ships' roles do not reveal this information. We know that John Gore, third lieutenant from Virginia, and James Magra, midshipman from New York, were on the first expedition. William Ewin, boatswain's mate from Pennsylvania was on the Second Expedition.

   Two Englishmen who sailed on the *Resolution* were to become famous. One was nineteen-year-old midshipman George Vancouver, who distinguished himself as commander of a voyage that charted the Pacific coast of North America (1791–1795). Vancouver had begun his training under Cook at the age of fifteen as a sailor on the second expedition. The other was master of the ship, William Bligh, who became notorious as captain of the celebrated Bounty at the time of its famous mutiny in 1789.
3. *Ibid.* 1521 (Cook to Sandwich).
4. The *Journals* contain the few surviving records of an extinct people. Tasmania became a penal colony in 1803, and in 1876 the last native Tasmanian died.
5. *The Journals of Captain James Cook* III, 79.
6. *Ibid.* III, 116.
7. *Ibid.* III, 108.
8. *Ibid.* III, 155.
9. *Ibid.* III, 199.
10. *Ibid.* III, 232, n., Williamson quoted.
11. *Ibid.* III, 1044, "Samwell's Journal."
12. *Ibid.* III, 232, n., midshipman Gilbert quoted.
13. *Ibid.* III, Bayly quoted, 134.

    Mai died about thirty months after the ships left, and the New Zealand boys died before Mai, "all of them of a natural death," according to a report given to Captain Bligh, who visited Huahine in 1789. *The Journals of Captain James Cook* III, 242, n.
14. *Ibid.* III, 256.
15. *Ibid.* III, Introduction, cxiii.

10 · Search for a Northwest Passage

1. Turtles could stay alive for months without being fed. They were stowed in ships as a source of fresh, delicious meat.
2. *The Journals of Captain James Cook* III, 269.
3. *Ibid.* III, Appendix III, King's Journal, 1392.
4. *Ibid.* III, 1418.
5. *Ibid.* III, 350.
6. Cook was convinced that "a very beneficial fur trade might be carried on with the Inhabitants of this vast coast, but unless a northern passage is found it seems rather too remote for Great Britain." *The Journals of Captain James Cook* III, 371.

   Although the fur trade was to benefit Russia and the United States primarily, at least five British ships arrived in 1786—two with men from Cook's third voyage.
7. *The Journals of Captain James Cook* III, Appendix III, King's Journal, 1426 SEE 1446 about Russians "Plundering & tyrannising over an helpless set of People."

   "The inhabitants of this Island are in a state of Subjection to the Russians & it should seem from what we observed amongst them that they are made to pay Tribute to their Masters, all of their Arms of every kind are taken away from them." Samwell's Journal, Volume III, 1142.
8. *The Journals of Captain James Cook* III, 420, n.1.
9. *Ibid.* III, 459.
10. *Ibid.* III, 449.
11. John Ledyard, *A Journal of Captain Cook's Last Voyage.*

    This book influenced New Englanders to trade with the northwest *after* the colonies became the United States.

    Ledyard attended Dartmouth College before signing up as a sailor in New London, Connecticut. He crossed the Atlantic twice before arriving in England. On July 4, 1776, he was on the *Resolution.* Had Ledyard known his countrymen were fighting a war against Britain, he probably would not have signed on.

    In 1786, encouraged by Thomas Jefferson who was then minister to France from the United States, Ledyard planned to hike across the continent from Nootka Sound to the east coast. Russian officers stopped him in Siberia, before he could cross over to mainland North America.

11 · Captain Cook, Hawaiian "God"

1. Maui, Kauai, Niihau, and Hawaii are Hawaiian names for their islands.
2. The humane Captain Cook was always worried that his men might spread venereal diseases. On many occasions he confined infected men to ship's quarters.
3. *The Journals of Captain James Cook* III, 479.
4. *Ibid.* III, 490–491.
5. *Ibid.* III, King's Journal, 503–504.
6. *Ibid.* III, 512.
7. *Ibid.* III, 512.

8. *Ibid.* III, 518, n.
9. *Ibid.* III, 519.

12 · The Killing of Captain Cook

1. *The Journals of Captain James Cook* III, 529.
2. *Ibid.* III, Samwell's Journal, 1196.
3. *Ibid.* III, 533, Clerke notations.
4. *Ibid.* III, 530, King quoted.
5. *Ibid.* III, 535, Phillips's Report.
6. *Ibid.* III, 536.
7. *Ibid.* III, 536, n.
8. *Ibid.* III, Samwell's Journal, 1200.
9. *Ibid.* III, 541.
10. *Ibid.* III, 542.
11. *Ibid.* III, 546, Clerke account.
12. *Ibid.* III, 1216, Samwell's Journal.
13. Some of Cook's bones were retained, kept in a heiau dedicated to Lono, and carried in annual religious processions. They disappeared when "idolatry" was forbidden in 1819.

13 · Homeward Bound

1. *The Journals of Captain James Cook* III, King's Journals, 669–670.
2. *Ibid.* III, Clerke, 697.
3. *Ibid.* III, Gilbert notes, 711.
4. *Ibid.* III, 1535. Benjamin Franklin: "To all Captains and Commanders of armed Ships . . ." (March 10, 1779).
5. *Ibid.* III, 1216, Samwell's Journal.

BIBLIOGRAPHY

Primary Sources

Banks, Joseph. *The Endeavour Journal of Joseph Banks*, 1768–1771, ed. J. C. Beaglehole, 2 volumes. Sydney, Australia, 1962.

Cook, James. *The Journals of Captain James Cook*, ed. J. C. Beaglehole. (Note: These volumes include journals and logs of officers and men on the voyages, letters, newspaper extracts, and numerous other documents.)
Volume I: The Voyage of the *Endeavour*, 1768–1771. Cambridge University Press, 1955.
Volume II: The Voyage of the *Resolution* and *Adventure*, 1772–1775. Cambridge University Press, 1961.
Volume III: The Voyage of the *Resolution* and *Discovery*, 1776–1780. Cambridge University Press, 1967.

Ledyard, John. *A Journal of Captain Cook's Last Voyage*. Photocopy of 1763 edition. Chicago: Quadrangle Books, 1963.

Secondary Sources

Beaglehole, J. C. *The Exploration of the Pacific*. Stanford University Press, 1966.

———. *The Life of Captain James Cook*. Stanford University Press, 1974.

———. "The Case of the Needless Death: Reconstructing the Scene—The Death of Captain Cook." See Winks, Robin, *The Historian as Detective*. New York: Harper & Row, 1968.

Cobbe, Hugh, ed. *Cook's Voyages and Peoples of the Pacific*. London: British Museum Publications Limited, 1979.

Conner, Daniel, and Millier, Lorraine. *Master Mariner*. Seattle and London: University of Washington Press, 1978.

Fisher, Robin, and Johnston, Hugh. *Captain Cook and His Times*. Seattle: University of Washington Press, 1979.

Halliday, E. M. "Captain Cook's American." *American Heritage*, December 1961.

Hough, Richard. *The Last Voyage of Captain James Cook*. New York: William Morrow, 1979.

Joppien, Rudiger, and Smith, Bernard. *The Art of Captain Cook's Voyages*. New Haven and London, Conn.: Yale University Press. Volume I, 1985. Volume II, 1985. Volume III, 1988.

Moorehead, Alan. *The Fatal Impact*. New York: Harper & Row, 1966.

Smith, Bernard. *European Vision and the South Pacific*. New Haven and London, Conn.: Yale University Press, 1985.

Wilford, John Noble. *The Mapmakers*. New York: Vintage Books, 1982.

Withey, Lynne. *Voyages of Discovery*. New York: William Morrow, 1987.

ABOUT THE ARTISTS

The artists who accompanied Captain Cook on his voyages left visual records of places they visited and peoples they encountered. Their drawings and paintings have artistic value, and are especially treasured because of the information they preserve.

Sydney Parkinson, son of a poor Scottish brewer, was chosen for the first voyage by Joseph Banks because of his ability to sketch birds, insects, and botanical specimens. He proved to be a superb artist. His portraits (e.g., pp. 19, 29, 31, 35, 39) and drawings (e.g., pp. 28, 33, 41) reveal a sensitive feeling for others and a keen eye for detail.

William Hodges, the official artist for the second voyage, was the son of a London blacksmith. Before joining Captain Cook's expeditions, he had earned a reputation as a landscape painter. Hodges's striking pictures of the Antarctic (pp. 57, 59), his fine portraits of natives (e.g., pp. 60, 67), and his poetic depictions of the Pacific Islands (e.g., pp. 62, 64, 65, 68) are invaluable achievements.

John Webber, son of a poor Swiss sculptor, was commissioned by the Admiralty to document the third voyage by drawing vivid descriptions of people and places (e.g., pp. 81, 83, 84, 87, 107). As a close companion to Cook, Webber was an observer and an active participant in dramatic events. Like Parkinson and Hodges before him, he enlarged people's vision of the world by revealing new, fascinating cultures.

The illustrations were selected by Rhoda Blumberg.

Illustrations on pages 24, 27, 29, 31, 33, 34, 35, 49, 61, 92, 94, 95, 96 (top), 104, 106, 107, 108, 114, 120, and 123 by permission of the British Columbia Archives and Records Service; page 37 by permission of the British Library; page 48 by permission of the British Museum; page 72 from the Castle Howard Collection; page 78 courtesy of His Excellency the Governor General of New Zealand; page 55 by permission of Lady Juliet Townsend, Oxfordshire, England; pages 2, 82, 84 (top), 89, 97, 99, 101, 105, and 117 courtesy of the Library of Congress; pages 57 and 119 courtesy of the Mitchell Library, New South Wales; pages 5, 18, 19, 36, 43, 46, 50, 59, 62, 68–69, 83, 87, 93, 96 (bottom), and 111 by permission of the National Archives of Canada; pages viii, 14, 23, 28, 39, 41, 54, 60, 67, 71, 79, and 115 by permission of the National Library of Australia; pages 3, 21, 56, 64, 65, and 124 by permission of the National Maritime Museum, Greenwich, London, England; page 9 by permission of the National Portrait Gallery, London, England; pages 7 and 74 by permission of the New York Public Library; pages 81 and 84 (bottom) courtesy of the State Library, New South Wales.

INDEX

Italicized page numbers refer to illustrations.

RHODA BLUMBERG "shines in the imaginative use of extensive research to tell, compellingly and entertainingly, stories from history," says *School Library Journal*. A self-proclaimed "compulsive researcher" who calls her library card her "most valuable passport," the author read Captain Cook's own journals as well as other primary and secondary source material before telling the story of his remarkable voyages.

Her masterful presentations of landmark events in history include *Commodore Perry in the Land of the Shogun*, a 1986 Newbery Honor Book, which also won the *Boston Globe/Horn Book* Award and the Golden Kite Award; *The Incredible Journey of Lewis and Clark*, and ALA Notable Book and Golden Kite Award winner; and *The Great American Gold Rush*, an ALA Notable Book that won the John and Patricia Beatty Award, presented by the California Library Association.

Accepting that award, Rhoda Blumberg said, "Stories are enchanting, and for me true stories—from history—are the most enchanting. History is a record of human behavior—the most fascinating subject of all."

The author and her husband, Gerald, live in New York State's Westchester County.

Blumberg, Rhoda.

The remarkable voyages of Captain Cook.

$18.95

DATE			